The Far End of the Park

James Casper

FarHaven press

PEQUOT LAKES, MINNESOTA

James Casper/Farhaven Press
4612 Hemlock Lane
Pequot Lakes, MN/56472
www.farhavenpress.com

Publisher's Note: This is a work of fiction. Names, characters, places, and incidents are a product of the author's imagination. Locales and public names are sometimes used for atmospheric purposes. Any resemblance to actual people, living or dead, or to businesses, companies, events, institutions, or locales is completely coincidental.

Book Layout and Cover ©2018 Kate Casper/TipTopWriting.com

The Far End of the Park/ James Casper. – 1st ed. revised
ISBN: 978-0-9994715-0-0 (Paperback)

To my loving wife Kate whose faith and work of days and hands bring this story to light at last

Note about the 40ᵗʰ Anniversary Edition

The Far End of the Park was written in 1977-78. Much has changed in the forty intervening years. Some things never change. A few updates, such as a computer taking over routines in Mr. Port's library, do not alter the landscape of a timeless story about a sensitive young man making his way down an uncertain path to a future somewhere beyond the far end of the park.

James Casper, July 2018

Contents

From this moment I began to conclude in my mind, that it was possible for me to be more happy in this forsaken solitary condition, than it was probable I should ever have been in any other particular state in the world...

—*Robinson Crusoe* by DANIEL DEFOE

1

An Orange Bus and a Yellow Ball

The boy leaned forward resting his arms on the back of a vacant seat. He peered through the bus's windshield where streaks had been left by a wiper clearing the last traces of a shower they had passed through a mile or so behind them. They had just turned onto a road of hard-packed sand with traces of scrubby grass running down its middle. Up ahead, hand-painted letters on a wooden sign welcomed them to Hawkers Park. The sign—more weathered than painted, more rotted than weathered—seemed more like a warning.

Out in the park, tourist kids had a ballgame going in a sunlit clearing not quite free of trees and humps. Shouts and screams would follow a yellow softball sailing through the leafy overhang between there and a row of small cabins. Anyone chasing after it might go tumbling over a gopher mound. Much of the time, a tree stood in the way, and what looked like a homerun ricocheted and rolled feebly across the infield. "Interference!" every player would shout as if they alone had thought of it. By prior agreement the batter took first, while other base runners could advance by one.

This had happened at least six times before what might have been an August calendar scene was ripped away to reveal September lurking behind it. An orange school bus pulled into the space between the first two cabins in a row of eleven, a school bus so out of place in August it seemed like a broken promise. What business had a school bus showing up at a time like this in a place where people took vacations, in the middle of a summer game just before supper?

Lightning could have struck the dog racing everywhere the ball flew, so suddenly did jaws drop and eyes glue themselves to a reminder nobody needed and the last thing anybody wanted to see. Thunder exploding overhead might soon bring an end to their game with two out and the lead run on second, but an orange school bus ended everything, piling the whole summer into a heap behind them with school sticking up over the top of it.

Eleven pairs of arms went limp, six on one team, five on the other. Eleven heads forgot the count of balls and strikes. The lone girl on the team of six stood frowning above the makeshift home plate, a square of floor tile. The runner on second strayed away from another floor tile to have a better look from the other side of a tree blocking his view. He might have been tagged by an alert baseman. Instead, no one noticed, no one bothered.

Squirrels stopped clambering through the treetops, parked themselves on convenient boughs, and appeared to stare. The dog whimpered and froze in a shaft of sunlight, still as a shaggy lawn ornament between home and first. Only a large lawnmower spun ahead as if nothing had changed. Driven by a man big enough to make it seem small, the lawnmower continued to clatter far down on the other end of the cabin row. It swept in circles around trees down that way and moved steadily closer.

Out of the bus stepped four people one by one, the first a slender man of angular features who could have come from a pillow fight, with his hair suggesting he'd been hit from several directions. His face seemed flushed. He rubbed his nose and scratched his head and returned the distant stares of the eleven ball players.

"Don't just stand there empty-handed, George," said his wife, who wore a red cap and blue jeans rolled up at the ankles, the next one out of the bus. She wrestled with a large cardboard box, a flap of which caught on the folding door as she flipped the whole thing sideways to get it through. From within, the silvery point of a clothes iron peaked.

Ignoring his wife, George dodged around her to receive an ironing board passed through the doors by the third of this group, a woman much smaller than the first, who let go of her end as soon as George had the whole thing in hand. She turned around and took a box from the arms of a boy, the last one coming out. The boy ducked back inside and appeared again, this time with two plump grocery bags pressed against his chest. At that moment, the ironing board opened of its own accord and sent George sprawling in front of the bus. Meanwhile Phyllis had gone ahead into the second cabin.

"Jeez," said George, rolling over and sitting there in fresh cut grass rubbing his forehead. "Jeez, I hate these things. Can't get them open when you want them to. Can't get them to stay folded up when they're supposed to." For George Cobb, life was a lot like that.

"I hope you didn't hurt anything," said the other woman, whose name was Kate, bending over him.

George, on his feet again, managed to say only his disposition had been affected.

It was clear to Kate and her son that he'd been drinking. They exchanged knowing glances as they went into the cabin where Phyllis was already emptying her box. Dish towels had been arranged near a sink. The iron stood upright on a green dining table.

"Welcome to your new home," said Phyllis, removing her cap and waving it around, as if the place, not much larger than a boxcar, was in fact an auditorium.

"Our new home," Kate repeated, trying her best to look pleased. George waltzed in, hugging the ironing board and covered with grass clippings.

"This isn't the way we help our friends move in—look at you, George!"

George, as his wife directed, did his best to look at himself. He peered between the ironing board and his chest, then down his trouser legs, both of them grass clippings the whole way, falling off in pairs and tangles on the floor. A grass clipping trail from there led back to the screen door.

The boy dropped his bags of clothing in a corner and went outside for another load. A parade had begun. Out of the school bus came everything he and his mother owned. Into the cabin it went, box and bag. Into a vacuum cleaner went the grass clippings. Soon it was over, and while the three adults sat inside drinking iced tea from a pitcher Phyllis had brought, the boy slipped outside around to the front of the cabin to watch what remained of the ballgame. Halfway up the cabin row the lawnmower clattered nearer. Thunder rolled, and rain drifted from a cloud scuttling along the horizon.

The boy turned on his tiptoes to peer in through the cabin window. His new home, viewed from out there, seemed much smaller than a boxcar even, no bigger than a rabbit hutch. Three people sitting at the kitchen table filled up most of what passed for space. Phyllis, the largest of the rabbits, looked up and waved at him. She pointed to a stack of plastic tubs with lids still in place—chicken, potato salad, beans, all fixed this morning. Soon they would eat, her gestures said. Come inside and feast, here in the rabbit hutch.

He couldn't hear her saying to the others what a great idea it was to move their stuff with her school bus, instead of the construction-company truck her husband had suggested. "Friends don't move friends around in dump trucks," she had pointed out to him earlier in the day when he was yet sober but no more sensitive than when he was drunk. Sensitivity was a quality George lacked, as far as Phyllis was concerned. *Sensitivity was something he needed help with.* Besides, using her school bus they had done it all in one trip, with no need to worry about rain. Hadn't they already passed through a shower, and wasn't it thundering just now?

The boy turned back to the ballgame with the lawnmower now near enough to drown out the shouts of players. In an opening through the trees he had an unbroken view of home plate where the girl was back at bat. At first viewed as a liability and so picked last when sides were chosen, she had proven herself the best slugger on either team. She had already taken down several branches and a pile of leaves with three hard line drives, the last of them nearly beaning a squirrel.

What happened next was one of those things that in retrospect seems to have occurred in eternity, rather than anywhere here on earth where the boy stood watching. The yellow softball, delivered underhand, floated toward her bat, which sprang from her shoulder to meet it. Before he ever caught a glimpse of it, the boy knew it flew his way, between the trees, as straight and true as an arrow aimed either at the window behind him or at his heart.

Eleven voices in a chorus sang, "Uh—Oh!" Eleven kids quit breathing, and time stood still.

He glanced at the man on the lawnmower, now only a few feet away, and then glanced back at the ball. His hand came up as far as he could reach in front of the window glass. The yellow ball hurtled into his palm with such force that he didn't have to tell his fingers to close around it. His knuckles driven back tapped the window pane. Phyllis, George, and his mother looked up from their paper plates. George said, "Jeez!" Out in the clearing, eleven cheers erupted. Eleven pairs of hands clapped. Even if you had trained all your life for such a moment, you still would have been surprised at such a catch as this.

He had hardly a second to enjoy it, and no chance to acknowledge their cheers by giving the ball a careless flip their way. He would have been nonchalant, as was his way, but a heavy hand fell upon his shoulder, and another grabbed the yellow ball.

"You kids should know better than play ball anywhere near these cabins," said the man who drove the lawnmower, not to those who'd been in the game at his back, but to the boy standing there a foot away, the one who hadn't been playing, who caught the ball and saved the window.

"You damned near broke this window!"

Out in the park, the game broke up. The cabin kids slunk away to their various cabins. The boy stood suddenly alone with his accuser, a big man wearing the sort of cap that boaters sometimes wear, white with an emblem above a black, pointed bill. A single gust swished through the park trees, dropping a few green acorns on the roof of the boy's new home. They rolled down over an eave, while overhead a rainbow arched in a brilliant wash of rainy sunshine, with the boy, the man, the tiny cabin, and the yellow ball centered beneath it, had there been anyone left in the park clearing to view it from there.

"What's your name?" demanded the man, even bigger now, standing so close the boy could smell the hamburger he'd recently eaten.

"Jude," the boy struggled to say.

"I'll remember that," said the man. "I never forget a name, and I never forget the face attached to it, and don't you forget what I just said. Do you hear?"

The unforgettable name and the unforgettable face attached to it didn't know whether to nod or shake its head, so it did both and swallowed hard, and that was the end for the time being.

The next morning when Jude came outside for his first full day in the park, he actually peered around the cabin corner before stepping fully into view. He half expected the man to be standing there still, waiting for him. Instead he found the yellow ball, slick with dew, lying beneath the window. As he picked it up and turned it over in his hand, he had the feeling he was at the beginning of something, and a long, long way from the end.

2

Perching in the Park

Jude was the name the big man said he wouldn't forget. The only child of Katherine and Philip Henley had the face he wouldn't forget.

When Jude was very young, his father—also very young as fathers go—died of a rare disease. Jude found its name as unpronounceable as the magic words of disappearing tricks and no easier to remember than his father who disappeared from his life, as if by trick, before he knew anything about him. He couldn't really forget him because he had nothing to remember, but he couldn't really ignore him either. His father was a room you could never go into in a house where you used to live. You couldn't help thinking about it and wondering what there was behind a door that never opened.

His mother's friends called her Kate. She was a frail, fidgety sort whose smoky blue eyes often seemed to gaze past him at something he could never see if he glanced back over his shoulder. Jude and his mother, being poor, moved around a lot, though they always lived in or near the northern town of Twin Rivers in summer tourist country.

They lived in an apartment over a hardware store with the light, oily smell of new tools in it and the sound of a bell ringing downstairs as customers came and went. They lived in a trailer house parked in a farmer's yard with white chickens under it all summer clucking and waking them up mornings and dusting themselves in its shade when the day grew warm.

They lived with Jude's grandmother the year she was sick and dying in a small brick house where framed pictures of his father stared at him from every shelf and shiny mahogany tabletop. In some of these—Jude fancied—his father seemed about to speak to him. His lips were tensed, words quivered there. Jude strained to listen, planting his elbows either side of the picture, resting his head in his hands, and gazing right into the eyes of the man they said was his father. Though minutes might go by with Jude struggling to keep his mind empty of any other thought, himself as motionless as the picture, he could never make out what his father was trying to say to him. His memory of this blended into another, of his grandmother in a rocking chair with a blanket over her lap and her chin nearly resting on her chest softly humming something he also couldn't make out, something as remote and far away as his father in another time. Jude was seven or eight.

He was fifteen the August evening Phyllis Cobb's orange school bus brought them to Hawkers Park, a tumbledown resort where city people stayed for their summer vacations, and only people who had nowhere else to stay and didn't mind cold drafts lived the rest of the year. Its cabins had been given the names of fish, game birds, and animals on hand-lettered wooden signs nailed up over their otherwise identical doorways. Since the cabins looked alike in almost every respect, without these signs to identify them, a stranger would hardly have known whether he slept in the *Bass*, the *Crappie*, the *Rabbit*, or the *Duck*. Nor would it have mattered. He might have slept in each of them on successive nights without knowing the difference.

Jude and his mother had moved into the *Perch*, second in the row through the park, a cabin with a squeaky screen door. This made it at least a little different from some of the others. In the *Pike*, first in the row, lived Harmon Grove, retired professional wrestler, owner of the cabins, creator of their doorway signs, and driver of the lawnmower. Tourists might have enjoyed these cabin names, and Harmon thought them clever, but Harmon had a high opinion of his own genius, and tourists came and went and didn't stay long enough to bother with their mail or much of anything else.

For the Henleys, though, *The Perch, Hawkers Park* had to be the address of their new home. It would even be written that way on Jude's records at school. They tried to make the best of this silliness. Kate began telling people they *perched* in a perch, as if they actually lived in the carcass of a fish, and even those who'd already heard her put it that way, laughed again. Whether because they thought it funny, or out of sympathy would have been hard to say.

"Why didn't he just put numbers on them?" she said, speaking of their new landlord as she sat at their kitchen table arranging a stack of envelopes one evening shortly after they arrived. "Then we would be in cabin two—that wouldn't sound so silly."

"Maybe he can't count," Jude suggested. By this time, he knew the big man on the lawnmower was their landlord Harmon Grove.

"Anything you can manage to laugh about will never get the better of you," Kate said, implying the next time her son felt like being critical, he might take this into account. "Well, anyway, I wish we were ducking in the *Duck*, instead—I really like ducks."

In what seemed no longer than a quack after that, the Duck was empty. In fact, all the other cabins were empty. Even before the Henleys had unpacked the last of their boxes, summer vacation season ended. Everyone who'd been playing ball the day Jude arrived had picked up their bats and their gloves and gone home for good, not gradually, but all at once as if in a Labor Day parade. He had only just learned their names, and now they were waving goodbye and calling him lucky for living in the park all winter long. Jude waved back and grinned and thought he wasn't lucky at all for being so alone.

It all happened so fast. If they hadn't left behind the old floor tiles marking home plate and the bases, Jude might have wondered if they had ever really been there, or if he had simply been dreaming, so quiet it suddenly was as he stood alone in the clearing and kicked second base. A week later, contemplating a fringe of grass growing up around home plate, he knew this was the last he'd ever see of them. He should have known better the moment they said, "See you next summer." He shouldn't have said it back to them.

Their parents would go somewhere else for next summer's vacation, and his brief companions of a fleeting August, a year older then, would find summer jobs and not even come along. With so much happening in their lives, why would they think about him, and why did people say things like *see you next summer* when it wasn't true, and they couldn't mean it? Maybe it was just too hard to say instead, *I'll never see you again—have a good life.* That's the way it really was. He'd be forgotten long before next summer came around.

But with so little happening in Hawkers Park, he was afraid he wouldn't forget *them* so easily. He wouldn't have anything else to think about, while they were thinking of so much else. Like it or not, he would go on remembering their names and even the tee shirts they wore the last time he saw them. Life from now on was bound to be that boring, or so he feared looking ahead, both through the imagined months of a school year just beginning and across the park clearing to the small cabin where his mother was even now preparing supper. For the first time, a wisp of smoke came from its chimney pipe, a sign of things to come.

Only places that had once been full of hubbub could have seemed as quiet as the park after Labor Day when the Bass and the Crappie were as silent as a taxidermist's fish. With nothing in particular happening out there, the *screech, screech* of the screen door grew louder as he went outside to look around. "A watched pot never boils," his mother sometimes said, yet there he was hanging around the other cabins regardless, scuffing up stones half buried in sand by their silent doorways, watching for something that never happened, like his school bus showing up on a holiday or like a pot that wouldn't boil. Soon this changed in what at first seemed a small way.

In early September, a local cabaret singer known as *Jeannie T* moved into the Woodcock, a twelfth cabin, one hidden from view on a forested hill on the end of the park farthest from theirs, so far and so hidden that weeks might have passed before Jude learned about it on his own. Instead his mother greeted him with the news when he arrived home from school on Friday of the first week at Twin Rivers High.

Though Jude wasn't much interested, she shared Jeannie T's story, as far as she recalled it. "I haven't heard of her in years. I always knew her as Jeanne Thorpe, but I suppose it's not a very good name for somebody in show business. I mean it does have a dull ring to it, doesn't it?"

While still known simply as Jeanne Thorpe, she had sung on a national television show, an amateur talent competition, when she wasn't much older than Jude.

"Few things ever got Twin Rivers people more excited. Such a big deal, Jude, you would hardly believe it. I suppose because she was so young and so very pretty, and nothing much ever happens around here ..."

Jude's mother rolled her eyes when she said this, as if to add that she herself was neither very young any longer nor very pretty. Jude, not thinking about Miss Thorpe but about nothing much ever happening, rolled his eyes too. He'd been so bored in the park he actually looked forward to school and was dreading the weekend ahead of him.

"When she left Twin Rivers with her parents on the train to New York City, her fans jammed the depot till its doors had to be flung open—though it was the middle of winter—and people spilled out into the street till that was blocked, and Twin Rivers had its first-ever traffic jam. Police were called in to straighten out the mess. The night of the talent show, extra television sets were brought into bars and cafés so everybody could see no matter where they sat. Nobody wanted to miss it."

"Did she win?" Jude asked, struggling to appear interested. "Did she win anything?"

"She won *something*, but it wasn't the top prize. I'm not sure what she won—it's been so long, almost twenty-five years ago. I was still in high school. Jude, it's funny the things we remember and the things we forget. It doesn't really have much to do with how important they seemed at the time."

At the time, as far as Jude was concerned, having Jeannie T living on the far end of the park mattered less than falling acorns pattering on their cabin roof just then. He was more likely to remember the acorns. He didn't think of the singer as a pot waiting to boil the minute he quit watching. He didn't think he would never forget her.

3

Big Fish and Little Fish

During the off-season, the months between Labor Day and Memorial Day, Harmon Grove made very little money renting his cabins. He kept the Pike for himself year around and spent winters in Florida. This year, departing from his practice of abandoning the park to its off-season fate, he had decided to hire a caretaker, so he placed an ad in the Twin Rivers newspaper, and the evening of the first day it appeared, hired Kate Henley for a salary amounting to half her rent.

He felt quite pleased with himself for thinking of this arrangement because he didn't really have to pay her anything and was instead profiting on the deal, for the Perch would have been empty otherwise. In fact, with somebody to be his eyes and ears all winter long, he might even rent some of the other cabins. It was enough to make him get up from his chair in the Pike, stroll to his bathroom mirror, and smile at himself.

Kate invited him to supper the September evening before he drove south in his green and white van. He appeared with a six-pack of beer and a loud greeting which he banged out as the Perch's screen door squeaked and slammed shut behind him.

Jude still hadn't grown accustomed to the sight of the lawnmower driver and his accuser from the day they moved in. During his first few weeks in the park, he had become adept at avoiding him, always managing to be on one side or one end of something, out of sight when Harmon was on the other. Cornered at last and unable to duck away, he was surprised to discover that the man who *never forgot a name and the face attached to it,* seemed to have forgotten him. Or at least he did a good job of feigning ignorance when Jude's mother, knowing nothing of the yellow softball incident, introduced them as if they were meeting for the first time.

"Well, how's things in the Perch?" he asked, ignoring Jude and popping open a can of beer even before he removed his red plaid jacket.

"As fine as I hope they are in the Pike," Jude's mother replied. She held a steaming bowl in her hands. Most people couldn't have touched it, but she held it in her hands while she asked Harmon Grove if he wanted a glass for his beer.

"Never use one," Harmon declared. "It's just another dish to wash. When you live alone as I do, when you're pushing fifty years old and don't have help with the dishes." (Here he glanced suspiciously at Jude.) "You're tight with the glassware. A can is good enough for me—thanks." He tossed his jacket across the back of an easy chair and sat down at the kitchen table before he was invited. He tilted his beer can into his face. When it came down, he had foam on his lips, and he asked if where he was sitting was okay.

"If you're happy where you are," said Kate, "we're happy to have you there."

Harmon was sitting where Jude usually sat. If his mother didn't mind, neither did he. It seemed a small thing to have this bully steal his chair and take his place at the table. It might have suggested to Jude that Harmon was taking over his life in other, unlooked for ways as well. He couldn't have foreseen that the man who had just taken his chair was about to drive a problem straight into the middle of their lives. So he didn't care that Harmon Grove took his place, and he hardly paid attention when the singer came into the conversation as mashed potatoes were being passed around behind the meatloaf and peas.

"Jeannie T they call her, but I call her *Thorpe*." Using the same inflection he might have used in calling someone a *dope* or a *loser*, he made it sound more like his opinion than her name. "She's in the Woodcock, as you know, way up on the other end," said Harmon, "and I wish she wasn't. It's a big mistake."

"What do you mean?" asked Kate.

"I mean she might fall behind with her rent. She might not pay it at all. After she moved in last week, I figured out she isn't working. She stays put most of the time. I don't see her going and coming the way people do when they have jobs." Harmon, who prided himself on being a keen ob-server of his fellowman—some might have said nosey—seemed to inflate as he said all this. He paused to let out a little of the air and self-esteem he had taken in. He waggled his fork over a gigantic mound of mashed potatoes.

"Maybe she has money saved," suggested Kate.

Harmon waved off that idea and dove into his mashed potatoes. "Anyone with money in the bank would be driv-ing a better car. Have you seen her car?"

Kate shook her head.

Jude had already seen it. "An old Buick?" he suggested.

"Exactly!" said Harmon. "It's a beater, a wreck. It sounds like a tractor, and it's got more rust holes than metal. And besides, if she had any money tucked away, she wouldn't ..." Harmon stopped to clear his throat and take a long drink of beer. When he came up for air, he left his sentence unfinished.

But both Jude and his mother knew what Harmon almost said—that people with any money didn't rent his cabins this time of the year. If they weren't down on their luck, they could find warmer places to spend their winters, bigger and more comfortable places. Since this applied to them as well as Jeannie T, he didn't say it. He wasn't being especially sensitive, but he didn't want to sour the good deal he'd made for himself by hiring this woman to live here with her punk kid.

Somewhere between the meatloaf and mashed potatoes and Jeannie T's old Buick, Harmon had decided Jude was an unreliable punk. He didn't like the look of him at all.

"Well, anyway, she has a pretty voice," said Kate who seldom criticized and always tried to put a best face on things.

"These days you need more than that," said Harmon himself favoring the worst face on things. "You need commonsense and luck, and if you ask me, Thorpe is short of both. I should never have rented to her. I should have asked her if she had a job and turned her down if she didn't. But, you know, I've got heart trouble." He tapped his chest over his heart with his beer can.

"I didn't know that, Harmon. I hope it isn't serious," said Kate. She either hadn't been listening closely and missed his meaning or had caught it and was mocking him.

"No, no," he said, grinning and brimming over with un-speakable fondness for his heart. "I mean it's too big. My heart is too big—that's my trouble. So I rented to Thorpe, even though I might lose money by it, but now I think I could lose more than I bargained for. There are limits to my generosity, and that's where the two of you come into this picture...."

Jude pushed a few peas around his plate with his fork. He stopped chewing.

"I want you to keep an eye on her while I'm away, a close eye, *every day*. It won't be easy with the Woodcock being the last cabin on the other end and almost out of sight from here, but you'll have to do it. I should have put her next door in the Bass. I shouldn't have put her anywhere."

He passed the peas around, as if they were *his* peas, and he was inviting the Henleys to have seconds. When Jude declined, Harmon detoured into the world of green vegeta-bles, how important it was to eat them and how much they had contributed to his wrestler's physique, second only to meatloaf it appeared, judging from the amount of that he had eaten and another portion he took aim at as he spoke. For good measure, he threw in some disconnected thoughts about children cleaning their plates and being grateful for the food they were given. Then he found his way back to Jeannie T and his heart trouble.

"I'll have Thorpe in court if she tries to pull anything on me. I'm a big-hearted man, but there's got to be a limit to it." He thumped his chest again with his beer can. Both might have been empty.

With all this said, between cans of beer, Harmon took a long, silent break to concentrate on his food. He ate his meatloaf in big hunks cut with the edge of his fork. With a piece of bread folded over and clutched in his free hand he mopped up the drippings on his plate. When he finished, it looked like plates that were still in the cupboard. Had it been his own cabin, in fact, where dishwashing was such a problem, it might have gone right back into the cupboard. He picked his teeth with his thumbnail, then gathered into his mouth from his shirtfront the crumbs of meat he'd dropped there. Likewise came a few peas from his lap.

Afterwards he tilted his chair back from the table, so far back that Jude couldn't see what kept it from crashing to the floor. Harmon had a way with their furniture which seemed meant to remind them that it was his, not theirs, just as with their cabin, as if they were his guests, here for the evening, and he not theirs. So he used their bathroom without asking first. He left a towel in the sink.

When he got back to the table, his lips still glistened with beef grease, his chest still heaved from the size of his heart. He sipped coffee between sips of beer and ate the last blueberry tart from a plate of four Kate set out for dessert.

"I hope nobody here minds if I help myself to this last tart," he said after he'd already devoured half of it.

It had been a three-cornered tart, folded over and scalloped like a seashell on its wide side, which was the side Harmon ate toward, successive bites forcing him to stretch his mouth wider and wider, until at last it vanished with berries squirting between slurps of coffee and beer. That concluded, he turned his attention to instructing the Henleys about their duties while he was in Florida. He sat up and shoved his dessert plate to one side. He spoke slowly and solemnly, with his elbows on his placemat.

"Thieves and burglars," he began, looking squarely at Jude as if he were an example of both. "Thieves and burglars see empty cabins in these summer resort areas as an easy target, so check all the doors and windows every day. If you notice anything wrong with them, call the sheriff. I mean if you discover a broken window or marks around a lock like somebody's been tampering with it—that sort of thing. Do you understand?"

Kate Henley nodded. Harmon stared at Jude till he nodded.

"There's not a lot in these places that anyone would want to steal," he said. He glanced around at the Perch's furniture, and then again fixed his gaze on Jude, "but sometimes crooks break in just to see if there's anything *worth* stealing."

Jude offered a suggestion. "Maybe you should put up a sign that says *Nothing Worth Stealing.*"

Harmon frowned, sensed sarcasm, but otherwise ignored this.

"A few years ago, a drifter broke into the Bass, and must have lived there most of the winter. Made such a mess of the place that I couldn't rent it the following summer." He paused and seemed to be doing a mental calculation of how much this had cost him.

Jude, already on the drifter's side, asked if they ever caught him. Harmon shook his head.

"He broke the legs off all the chairs, and for some reason, he sawed the bed in two. The sheriff never caught up with him. Of course by the time I reported it, he could have been a thousand miles away, which is where the two of you come in. If anything happens around here, I need to know lickety-split." Again he looked at Jude, then his mother while pointing to a can of beer he had slid toward her side of the table.

She declined this with a flick of her hand, reached down into her purse hanging from the back of her chair and pulled out another cigarette. A blue tissue came with it and fluttered to the floor.

Harmon forged ahead. "Then you've got to watch the roofs. Most years it never gets warm enough to melt much of the snow before spring comes, so it piles up on the roofs all winter, and it will warp 'em as sure as I'm sitting here if you don't sweep it off now and then with a long-handled broom I'll bring over tomorrow morning before I head out."

He looked at Jude's mother, and she nodded, then at Jude till he nodded again.

"Last of all, there's that Thorpe woman," he said sounding distinctly vicious. "I shouldn't have rented to her in the first place, but done is done, ain't it?"

Kate nodded while inhaling deeply of her cigarette. Her eyes crossed, focusing on the glowing end of it.

Harmon didn't look at Jude this time. Instead he extended his arm—a limb that might have been a tree limb from which a swing could hang—and laid a heavy paw on Jude's shoulder. Harmon hadn't read books about body language and gentle touches expressing sincerity. He hadn't this in mind at all. No, his wrestling days had taught a different, harsher lesson. Whatever passed for sincerity in it was simply the clear intention to rip somebody's head off. Body contact achieved control over people, in the present instance control especially over a modern-day boy whose interests probably weren't healthy, whose brain probably wasn't reliable, and who seemed at times to be making fun of him, a punk in other words.

"I want you to walk up to the Woodcock every day and make sure Thorpe isn't sneaking out with her clothes and stuff. Your mother can't be expected to do it—it's too far. But it isn't too far for you. *Every day*, do you hear? Walk all the way up there and get a good look at what's going on."

His paw tightened on Jude's shoulder.

"And if you ever see her moving out, or if you don't see any sign of her at all for a few days and think she's already gone, come running right back here and tell your mom—and you call me, Kate."

His grip tightened a little more.

"I'll be leaving my Florida number with you." He glanced around the cabin as if Jude's shoulder were the farthest thing from his thoughts. "Looks like you don't have a phone," he said.

"No phone," said Kate snuffing her cigarette in a saucer and nodding toward the spot where a phone might have been, a tiny hole in the wall to her left with three colored wires protruding.

"Well, no matter," said Harmon. "You can always call me from the pay phone up on the highway."

Jude's arm was falling asleep now, his fingers tingled, a hot cramp spread up from his neck to his ear.

"I can't kick her out between November and April, even if she doesn't pay her rent. It's the law in this state—no cold weather evictions—so I'm stuck with her. But if we catch her sneaking out without paying up or at least making arrangements to pay, that's different, that's against the law too. I can bring the sheriff in," Harmon was saying, squeezing. "We'll catch up with her. You can bet on it."

Jude hollered and tumbled out of his chair.

"What's the matter with you?" Harmon stared down at him. His face feigned surprise, though not so well that it concealed the smile curling at the corners of his lips. This punk wasn't very tough either.

"You were hurting my shoulder," said Jude.

"That's not it," said Harmon. "You probably ate too fast." He reached down, grabbed Jude by the arm, and yanked him to his feet.

Jude couldn't believe his strength. Kate, who had jumped from her chair and was biting her lip, couldn't believe his manners. But neither of them said so.

"I'm okay now," said Jude exchanging glances with his mother.

"Of course you are," chortled Harmon.

He repeated his opinion that it all came from eating too fast, though he knew, and Jude knew—and Jude's mother could hardly have doubted—that not chewing between bites wasn't the reason.

Into her eyes had come the look of looking at things far away. Jude seeing this said again he was okay, but even this reassurance could not bring her back. Though his neck still ached and his fingers seemed pricked by a hundred pins, not for the world would he have let her know, not as long as her eyes looked that way. How could she rely on him if the likes of Harmon Grove made him squeak? He would have to be stronger in the future than he'd proven to be today.

"A boy growing up without a father needs somebody to teach him about being tough," said Harmon as if he'd had enough of this game and had just read Jude's mind.

This wasn't the first time Jude had heard it: a sentence starting with *a boy growing up without a father* ... could be either sympathetic or critical and end in many ways, none of them good and all of them elaborating on something he lacked. A boy growing up without a father *must feel lonely, needs guidance, needs a male model, has too much on his shoulders, grows up too fast, doesn't grow up fast enough, is bound to get into trouble*, etc. But this was the first time he'd heard about being tough. What was he supposed to do, pick fights with people because he didn't have a dad?

Harmon pushed himself away from the table, stood up, and put on the boating cap he'd kept on his knee while he ate. A piece of tart popped out of it and landed on the floor.

Jude hated him—why did the jerk need to bring his father into it? It was already bad enough.

Meanwhile Harmon felt like having another satisfying look at himself in the mirror as soon as he got home. He enjoyed giving painful instruction, especially to disrespectful punks like the kid whose name he'd already forgotten again. He sauntered home triumphantly to cabin one, the Pike, the predatory fish. He swung from his hand by its plastic strapping the two remaining cans in his six-pack.

A few elm leaves had blown in around Harmon's feet when he opened the Henley's' door which he hadn't bothered to close on his way out. When Kate closed it, they fluttered under the kitchen chairs. The leaves were yellow.

Their floor, a pattern like the flannel shirt Harmon wore that evening, was green linoleum squares.

Parting a curtain, Kate looked after him. Jude came to her side and peered out with her. A golden river of setting sun flooded the yard between their cabin and Harmon's, between the Perch which was a little fish and the Pike which fed upon perch. It was a scene much too lovely for the figure passing through it, too lovely for the evening just ended. But the owner of Hawkers Park was not a mere predatory fish. He was a big, shaggy man who from the back resembled a bear, and over the long tree shadows falling across their yard he shambled like a bear upon logs in a golden stream. He could not possibly have deserved to be so happy.

"He sure ate like he enjoyed everything," Kate said. "I mean he isn't delicate, but I suppose we could take his eating as a compliment."

"He ate two tarts," Jude said into the window with his breath fogging it. "I didn't eat too fast. Thorpe may be broke and not very lucky, but I'm glad she's going to be living here this winter and not him." It didn't strike him as strange to be taking the side of someone he'd never met.

"Call her *Miss* Thorpe, Jude. Don't say it his way."

Miss Thorpe it would be from then on, *Miss Thorpe* or *Jeanie T*, but thanks to Harmon, never again just plain *Thorpe*, his way.

At that moment, as if he knew they would be staring after him, Harmon looked back and waved. Jude's mother drew away from the window, with her hand out to return his wave as the curtain fell into place between them.

"I don't like to be caught staring at people," she whispered. "I don't suppose he meant to hurt you. They say years ago he was a professional wrestler and pretty good at it. That's how he made his money, so now he can spend winters in Florida. He's a big man, stronger than he knows perhaps. Try to accept that. He's been good to us—he didn't have to rent this cabin either—and we can live here for a lot less than anywhere else this winter."

She quickly turned away from Jude, but not before he noticed her crimson face. He didn't know whether it was embarrassment or her anger he wasn't supposed to see.

"If the guy was a wrestler," said Jude, "he knows how strong he is, Mom, and you know he's a total jerk."

She wasn't about to admit that she agreed.

Don't be so quick to judge people, she sometimes said to him when he complained about somebody, a teacher or a classmate, but not this time. Instead her foot nudged one of the yellow leaves skittering in behind Harmon. She stooped to retrieve the blue tissue that had fallen from her purse, and then lit another cigarette.

"Winter is coming fast," she said to change the subject. "It's getting dark already."

"Yes," Jude said, without giving much thought to the evidence of dead leaves on their floor and darkness at their windows. Instead he was wondering how he would learn to be tough and how long it would take.

He could feel a change coming though, a chill in the air and a lengthening darkness having little to do with weather and the time of year it was. His life had slowed down like a car turning a corner before taking him off in a new direction. He couldn't see where it was taking him, but he knew it was somewhere he had never been.

His mother at the table again snuffed her half-smoked cigarette in an ashtray. She too could read his mind. "Give yourself time, Jude. Don't make too much of things that don't really matter."

But what did matter was more basic even than his young man's wounded pride and his instinct to protect his mother. When your father dies before you can remember him, you almost never feel sad about it because you never knew what it was like for him to be alive, and so you can't get your thoughts around this emptiness. But at this moment Jude *could* get his thoughts around something. He thought of his father being dead before he could teach him about things he needed to know, and he hated Harmon for assuming he could take his father's place teaching him a lesson, and forgetting the other pains he felt, he felt sad.

4

Rainy Daze

Harmon backed out of his driveway, honked his horn to announce his departure, and pointed his green and white van toward Florida. Alone in the cabin called the Woodcock and out of sight—at least for as long as leaves remained on the trees—Jeannie T was practicing her songs.

Jude's school bus heading north out of Twin Rivers at the end of the day met Harmon's van heading south. Sitting in his usual seat on the left a few rows back, gazing out a window, Jude actually saw it go by with a mound of Harmon's belongings wrapped in a blue tarp tied up on top and Harmon, another mound, behind the wheel. An hour later he slipped into a small clearing behind the Woodcock, ducked down behind a fuel oil tank, and for the first time heard Jeannie T singing through her cabin's thin walls.

He couldn't have repeated a word of the one song he heard halfway through before he jumped up and raced away. At what seemed a safe distance from the base of a hill he looked back over his shoulder where the Woodcock might have been seen except for trees in the way, and where Jude might have been seen from the Woodcock except for those same trees. He swallowed hard as if something he'd been chewing could finally go down. He inhaled for what seemed the first time. A sense of adventure mixed with fear, a sense of duty with regret, and a sense of putting something behind him with another of how much lay ahead.

A routine had begun, and within a week Jude settled into it. He would stay behind the Woodcock longer than he had to. In full view, he would pause to examine a strange red mushroom growing near the base of a birch clump mere steps from the cabin's back wall. He would shuffle home to the Perch, not run.

Jeannie T sang a few songs Jude had heard before, but many hardly anybody younger than his mother could remember. They struck him as strange and sad-sounding at first, but because she sang them so often, and he heard them so much in the passing weeks, he soon had them comfortably by heart without really trying. With the sun setting, he would walk home through the last shadows of the day and report to his mother.

"Miss Thorpe is singing like always," he would say.

Somehow, perhaps because it was the last thing Harmon would have called her, they had gotten in the habit of calling her *Miss Thorpe* whenever they talked about her.

"Good," Kate Henley would say as if Jude's report was the best news of the day.

In the early going, before this became routine for both of them, she occasionally had more to say.

"She's just like a bird on the far end of the park singing all day when the summer birds have flown away."

Jude liked the way his mother put that. He felt better about Jeannie T and her peculiar old songs when he thought of her staying around through all seasons of the year like a bird that never left you.

Because his father was gone forever, Jude grew up valuing such things.

The Woodcock stood apart from the other cabins on its forested hill around a bend in the sandy road running along one side of the park. It had pine siding stained to look like redwood, a mute gray shingled roof, and windows trimmed the same dark brown of all the park cabins. Summers you wouldn't have noticed it up there, except by a chance glance from just the right angle, or if you had known where it was to begin with, and so knew exactly where to look through the trees. Winters, when the trees were bare, save for a few red oaks, it stood out on its hilltop and seemed the most conspicuous thing around, once you got far enough down the sandy road that the other cabins had slipped out of sight around the bend.

On the west side from Jeannie T's hill was a strip of woods, the sandy township road, and beyond that more woods and meadows, both wild places and pastured ones with barbed wire tacked haphazardly to trees and sometimes a soggy, bedraggled horse or two standing aloof in the drizzle. Jude seldom approached from this side as long as enough daylight remained after school and before winter set in with its deep snow blocking his other way. A path through the park gave him a better, less conspicuous trail to circle between the Perch and the Woodcock every afternoon.

Jeannie T didn't have a choice. Her steep driveway, an obstacle course of clay ruts, trees, and protruding boulders, was an accident waiting to happen as she came and went, which wasn't often as far as he could tell—Harmon was right about that. If Jude happened to spot her, driving in or leaving, he couldn't watch without thinking she might lose control and wreck her car. What was he supposed to do then, run up to Twisters, and call the sheriff?

If Harmon Grove's heart put her in the Woodcock, Jude decided, it wasn't the large and generous heart Harmon bragged about, but a mean and thoroughly metallic one, a heart that might have let her live in any of the other cabins, as long as they were empty anyway, but sent her here and didn't care if she broke her neck. Harmon's only regret had been that it wasn't quite so easy to spy on her now. This was Harmon's heart, as hollow as an empty beer can.

Jude's autumn footpath led him along the edge of a ravine behind the cabins. A river ran through this ravine, fast enough when its waters were high that its trickling and gurgling could be heard by anyone passing along the path above, though it couldn't be seen in any season. The ravine was deep, and its sides densely overgrown with oaks, hazel shrubs, basswoods, and willows leaning into the gulch. The ravine was called Hawkers. Its noisy river was the North Crow, especially noisy this season, in fact a flood.

One of Jeannie T's songs had to do with rainy days. She often sang it, and as if by magic, the more she sang it, the more it rained. It rained so often that Jude thought about slipping a song request into her mailbox.

Sing about sunny weather instead, his note would have said. Then maybe his feet wouldn't get wet, and so many leaves wouldn't drip on his head. Instead his feet got wetter and more leaves dripped, and when they fell they didn't flutter but dropped in precise circles under their own trees, mats of the same leaf and the same color. Swatches of red, orange, and yellow lay before Jude as he walked along, with his footsteps sometimes leaving a trail of one color leading to the next.

Between showers, the sun and wind dried what it could, erasing the colored circles, erasing his trails, mixing up the colors. He walked through this as well, through wet turning dry and dry turning wet again, and always with his head full of thoughts till sometimes he wished it was like a radio, and he could just push a button and turn it off or at least find another station.

As the season wore along, rainy days finally gave way to dry, windy ones, and stayed that way, while the end of October neared. Drifts of leaves curled around the Woodcock till the base of its fuel oil tank and even its concrete block foundation sank out of sight beneath them.

Jude had been up there every day at this point, an unbroken string of more than fifty days, in the course of which he began to think of himself more as a lookout than a spy, and even more on Jeannie T's side than on Harmon's where he could never have been in the first place.

This was an even bigger change than from wet weather to dry. Harmon was months from returning, and the whole winter lay between him and the woman he called *Thorpe*. She was safe enough from him and his suspicions. Yet as the days grew shorter and dark came sooner up there on the hill, he was keeping an eye out for Harmon to come back, not for Jeannie T to go away. It had all flipped around. Any sign of him, and he thought he might have run straight to her door to warn her.

He pictured such things while listening to her songs, crouched behind the Woodcock by its oil tank. He didn't have to stay longer than to hear a note or two, a word or two, enough to tell him she was there, but having come so far, he sometimes lingered. A window nearby, the only one in the back wall of the cabin, was always closed and looked as though it had never been opened in the history of Hawkers Park. A faded blue corduroy curtain drawn across it added to this impression. He soon quit worrying she might look out some afternoon. Had she done so and discovered him, he imagined telling her he was only there for her sake. It wouldn't be a lie since that was how he felt. *Harmon's still in Florida*, he would say. *Don't worry*. After his first few visits he even quit crouching behind the fuel oil tank. He would lean back carelessly against her cabin wall, take in the hilltop view, and never give a thought that she might discover him there.

The Woodcock might have had the worst of cabin driveways, but none of the others had its view. Climb the highest tree in the rest of Hawkers Park, stand on its very top craning your neck and you wouldn't see half as much as you could see from where Jude stood every afternoon. On its east and north sides, he could follow the North Crow's meandering course as it cascaded out of Hawkers Ravine into broad, grassy marshlands beyond. The part of these marshes closest to him had become a flood pool this autumn. But farther away in the very distant distance the North Crow seemed to be no more than a blue and silver wisp curling away from him till it narrowed and vanished. From there, Jude's eyes could roam out over more miles of marshland sprawling before him.

His imagination also roamed. Prodded by the singer's strange, sad songs and his own isolation, it roamed wildly and sometimes much farther than he wanted to go, till he seemed to be in a trance, awake and yet dreaming.

One murky afternoon with the distant marshlands receded behind a gauzy veil, he imagined walking around to the front of the Woodcock and seeing all the way to Twin Rivers High School with its football team practicing for homecoming while cheerleaders cart-wheeled on the sidelines. It was all as plain and clear to him as if he'd been gazing down on the athletic field from a sunlit window in the school, not sitting cross-legged by a rusty oil tank looking down at a moth fluttering in a patch of moist grass just beyond his knees.

Was this what it felt like to be going crazy? It was enough to make him stand up, shake himself, and race home down the hill. He might call someone when he got there, a school friend, the first person he could think of to talk to about *anything* that would make him seem normal again. He was still imagining things. They didn't even have a telephone in the Perch. He stood by the colored wires coming through a hole in the wall, pretending he held a phone, trying to think of someone he might call, trying to think of something to say, and trying so hard not to be crazy he almost wanted to cry.

"Supper's ready," his mother said.

This snapped him out of it. He was like a swimmer soaring up from a dive into a deep pool. He flipped his head as if to clear water from his eyes and ears. Rain pattered on their cabin roof, steam rose from a kettle, he was home again.

"Jude," his mother was saying, "would you set the plates out? How's Miss Thorpe this afternoon?"

5

A Long Short Day

Jude had become perhaps the only teenager in the world who knew Jeannie T's old songs by heart. He learned from this that knowing something you never wanted to know can be a burden. A jack-in-the-box tucked inside you, it could pop out any time.

Around Twin Rivers High School where he was in the tenth grade, he forgot himself and hummed a tune he'd heard her practicing the day before for what seemed the hundredth time. This happened in Mr. Martin Evanson's geometry class while he worked on problems at the end of chapter six. Triangle problems were arrayed like boat sails across the page, a flotilla catching the breeze, drifting, and taking Jude's mind along for the ride.

It was the last hour of the day, the last day of October, Halloween and a time for tricks, and Mr. Evanson with his fingers in his moustache stood in the doorway like a gray-ing, preoccupied deception, a trap. He leaned back against the frame and appeared to have his thoughts elsewhere. His brown eyes roamed absently over the lowered heads of his students to the classroom clock and then from there out to the empty hallway and down it a dozen lockers and a door or two, then back to the clock, as if he shared with his young geometers a limp impatience to be done with this day. *As if.*

"Psst. What's that song you're humming?" whispered Mandy Gordon who sat to Jude's right in the fifth row from the door and Mr. Evanson.

Jude hadn't been aware he was humming anything. It had just slipped out, the way songs will when you've heard them a lot—you don't even have to like them. He never expected to be asked about it, but the curiosity of Mandy Gordon, once aroused, could not be sidestepped. Besides, her pretty face and long, auburn hair were hard to ignore. He whispered back to her the name of Miss Thorpe.

"Who?" said Mandy, raising her voice because here was a name she didn't recognize, and she thought she knew everybody living anywhere around Twin Rivers.

"Jeannie T," Jude ventured, "*Jeanne Thorpe*—people waved to her from bridges," the part of his mother's story he most vividly recalled.

"What?" said Mandy, still loud.

Then Jude told her how she lived alone in a cabin on a hill, singing her songs every afternoon. "Practicing, I guess you'd say."

"*Alone? Those* songs? *Every day?*" Jude nodded.

"Boy, how weird!"

Swelling out from between Mandy's lips, a purple pearl of bubble gum lightened into lavender, then shrank back into her mouth without breaking. Her mouth was fruity, her face infinitely more interesting than Mr. Evanson's triangles, even if there were—as Mr. Evanson had reminded them—an infinite number of triangles and here only one Mandy. When she leaned closer to him across the aisle, he could make out designs on a clip holding her hair back above a small, crustacean pink ear from whose lobe glinted a tiny blue star and a golden bangle. Her perfume took his breath away.

Because she was a basketball cheerleader and he not in sports at all, she usually ignored him. No, it was worse than that—if she had actually ignored him, there might have been in her manner some sense that he existed. Instead Jude was invisible. He didn't exist. Had he been a block of wood in her path, she at least would have stepped around him. In Mandy's path, he was simply empty space. If he somehow managed to get her attention, she would look at him as if he were very far away, and she ought to have binoculars to see who he was. But this afternoon she made him feel close, just as close as they really were. He felt tremors in the various kinks of his digestive tract.

All the same, she annoyed him by calling the singer *weird*. It wasn't a fair word, he thought. It didn't fit her, as far as he was concerned, and Mandy shouldn't have used it to describe somebody she had never met. He was about to argue the point with her when the wandering, preoccupied eyes of Martin Evanson glided back in from the hallway, swept like a dust cloth over the classroom clock, and fastened squarely on the two of them, instantly losing their preoccupation.

"Let us all hear," he chirped.

It was Jude's turn to ask, "What?"

"You know very well what I mean—you, too, Mandy. We all want to hear what both of you have to say since it's so important that it can't wait."

A few of Mandy's friends exchanged grins over Mandy caught flirting with Jude Henley of all people.

This was too much. "He was just humming some weird song," said Mandy. She swallowed her gum and glanced accusingly at Jude who seemed far away again, teetering on the edge of non-existence.

Twenty faces in the first four rows had turned from triangles to stare at Jude. The grin on every face was prophetic, for Mr. Evanson said, "I was just now wishing I could hear a song. What better way to end the day?"

He wore a sweater the color of Mandy's gum, a smile as fruity. He folded his arms across his chest. He was playing the oldest trick every teacher knows, and like every teacher who ever tried it, he was acting as if it had never been tried before, and he must be brilliant for having thought of it first.

"Come up here and sing us your weird song, Jude."

A single whoop heralded an even noisier, more obvious silence when nobody joined in. The classroom clock said two minutes to three, two minutes till school was out for the day. A giggle sputtered from somewhere behind Jude and then came a single clap from hands out of sight under a desk top. With every eye in the class upon him, Jude turned his own to triangles. He suddenly loved looking at them. He couldn't imagine neglecting triangles for very long, and he hoped everyone else felt the same.

"We're all waiting," chimed Mr. Evanson just as Jude began to think he'd given up. "Come up here and sing for us."

Jude loved sitting at his desk. He couldn't tear himself away from triangles. He was thrust at from behind by rough hands from the sixth row, the hands of Mandy's basketball players.

Who has any friends at moments like this?

He staggered to his feet and was pushed forward by other hands and arms along the way. He mounted a platform in front of the room and stood to the pencil-sharpener side of Mr. Evanson's desk. Isolated there, slightly elevated and silent, he faked indifference, while a frown from Mr. Evanson, peeping in and out from the curving ends of his moustache, quelled laughter, hoots, applause, and a belch.

One minute to three.

"We're all waiting," Mr. Evanson said again. "We're holding our breaths with anticipation." His sweater seemed to inflate with all the anticipation he inhaled, a vast unnecessary quantity of it.

Jude stared at his shoes. He stared out a window where a janitor in gray coveralls was lowering the schoolyard flag. Its halyard pulley clanked against the pole as Jude opened his mouth and pondered the ceiling, a dry, dirty ceiling, but not much drier than his mouth just then, nor less likely to produce a sound, nor dirtier than the trick being played on him.

Thirty seconds of the school day remained, a mere thirty seconds and the tiniest sliver of time to stab him till it hurt. The clock's sweeping hand disappeared with his gaze upon it. Mr. Evanson had sauntered in from the doorway to take it off the wall and hold it behind his back.

This in itself was quite amazing since none of them knew that Twin Rivers High classroom clocks were simply hanging there and could be removed so easily. In circumstances less sensational, this distraction might have saved Jude. As it was, a couple of classroom pranksters made mental notes before Mr. Evanson resumed his attack.

"You won't get away with stalling. This day will end with a song—it won't end any other way." He held the clock out for an instant and then slipped it back behind him. More mental notes were taken.

"Come on, Baby, sing to us!" squealed Peter Johnson, perennially condemned to the first row for his habit of such outbursts.

"Shut up, Peter, or this will be a duet!" said Mr. Evanson in a low, threatening tone.

Ronny Faber laughed.

"A trio, a quartet, a quintet, a chorus if need be!"

Whatever control Mr. Evanson won over his class with these threats, he seemed to lose over himself. He had taken on the features of a wild animal trainer, pointing to right and left with full-length gestures of his free arm, dancing on the balls of his feet with his legs far apart, attacking, withdrawing, attacking again, and all the while holding the clock out of sight.

"We're waiting for your song, my friend."

Jude wanted to protest that he wasn't Mr. Evanson's friend, that the song was Jeannie T's—not his—and that he'd learned it by accident and hummed it that way. These were the facts. To say so would have been his first choice, but instead he opened his mouth and ended his misery the only way he could by croaking out a line just as the three o'clock bell rang outside in the hall.

Off key and way too fast, he sang about days growing shorter when you reach September. On this late October day they should have been even shorter, but croaked or sung, fast or slow, on key or off, the words didn't seem true at all.

Classmates on both sides rose as if a giant wave had just passed beneath them. A tide of laughter and slamming geometry books rolled toward Jude. In row five, Mandy Gordon leaped up and yelled with her hand cupped beside her mouth, cheerleader fashion. Behind her the basketball players waggled their long arms over their heads and cheered. Since he couldn't think of anything else to do, Peter Johnson shoulder-punched Ronny Faber. Time, the clock, was back on the wall.

"Oh, Baby, oh!" Peter groaned ecstatically, coiling up from his seat while Ronny punched him back.

Mr. Evanson, his Halloween trick played, waved in disgust as this clamor roared past, flooded into the hall, and became a clatter of banging locker doors. Brushing past Jude, Mandy Gordon said to everyone within earshot, "Boy is this kid weird!" Her words immobilized him on the desk platform till Mr. Evanson drew near and laid a pudgy hand on his shoulder. They were alone in the room now.

"Sorry, Jude," he said. "We can't have commotion in the room—you understand that, I'm sure."

"I'm sure," Jude repeated, though not in the same tone he'd heard it. Mr. Evanson himself had caused most of the day's commotion.

"We're still friends, aren't we?" Mr. Evanson's question sounded rehearsed from an education textbook on school discipline. *First pain, then pleasure give*—Chapter Six. With pain behind them now, the thought of Mr. Evanson's friendship was supposed to be pleasure.

Jude didn't answer, except to say that he had to go to the lavatory.

"Where did you ever pick up that old song?" asked Mr. Evanson, chatty, not giving up. Chapter Seven—*Getting things back to normal.*

Jude shrugged and stepped off the platform, out from under the pudgy hand, out of the room.

There seemed to be nothing going his way this Halloween afternoon in the dreary, crowded hallway of Twin Rivers High with lockers still banging and purple gum bubbles swelling out between lips on all sides, and Peter nearby still shoulder-punching Ronny Faber, and Ronny ducking and punching back. The school had its rules prohibiting all such things, but Mr. Evanson turned his back in disgust, and Principal Desmond Willoughby was in a distant corner of the gym inspecting a leaking water pipe. At this moment nothing mattered quite as much as celebrating the spectacle of Jude. There wasn't a rule against that.

Mandy Gordon had called him *weird.* It was like a cheer she was leading. This meant that her homely friend Luanne would also call him weird. There already was Luanne, just two steps away—the inevitably homely best friend of a pretty girl—standing beside her at the locker they shared and grinning just now till her molars showed. The entire basketball team would join in, and so would Luanne's younger brother, who crossed his eyes when Jude passed him in the cafeteria lunch line next day. They'd all call him weird.

While Jude elbowed his way one direction down the hallway, Mr. Evanson went the other, to the faculty lounge where he went in, closed the door behind him, and said to Miss Constance Greshmer, the art teacher, "I've had a god

-awful day." He almost always said this at the end of a day. "Just plain god-awful."

"What a shame!" Connie Greshmer almost always replied.

"It all comes from having geometry scheduled for the last hour. It's *the worst thing imaginable*." He sat down at a table where Miss Greshmer was rearranging items in her purse. He laid a pudgy hand on her arm. This wasn't a romantic gesture, for Mr. Evanson had read in a recent bestseller that body contact was important, that it implied sincerity and encouraged empathy. That's why he laid his hand there. Miss Greshmer had a late-flowering case of acne—the worst thing *she* could imagine.

The worst thing Jude could imagine was his weird reputation, how having sprouted now, it would take root and grow and spread like a vine across his path, tripping him up at every turn and finally overwhelming him. He had always gotten along in school by keeping out of sight in the main pack where he wasn't noticed. Nobody ever thought of him when class presidents and carnival kings were nominated. If sides were chosen for teams in gym class, he was never captain. He was always chosen in the middle somewhere, never last, never first. He wanted it that way. He liked being inconspicuous, out of the spotlight, playing minor roles in class plays, having teachers who never learned his name before Halloween and always forgot it over the summer. So he had shuffled along till this Halloween day, with nobody thinking of him as a winner or a loser or as anything at all in particular, least of all weird.

Now everything had changed. For the first time in his life, he was aware of something within himself he would have to hide from people who couldn't understand it. He saw this in a way, and perhaps felt it more than saw it, as the school day ended with his ears burning long afterwards and his thoughts a tangle of embarrassment, regret, and anger.

What he failed to see was something like a highway sign with a curving arrow on it cautioning him about the road ahead. He had Miss Thorpe's old songs by heart, but he was only beginning to learn that whatever you have by heart— even if you don't want it—has you by heart as well.

6

Checked Out Without Checking

With Twin Rivers High School's last bell of the day still echoing in the halls, Jude ran downstairs to the school library to check out some books in the five minutes before it closed. He didn't care what the titles were, just as long as they were books—books to take with him on the ride home, when he might need to hide his face in one and pretend not to hear, if it came to ignoring the teasing he expected. He saw a downpour of that coming, thanks to Mr. Evanson, and books would be his umbrella.

In the street, just outside the library window, his school bus was already loading. Half of it stood in the window above the aquarium, half of it in a window above the card catalogues. Both halves were the same used only weeks before to move Jude and his mother into the Perch. He grabbed a red book and a green book from a shelf near the world globe, and twirling the globe in passing, he ran to the checkout desk where he took a yellow book from a wire rack. He didn't bother about titles. He didn't care what they were any more than if you were ducking down behind a shrub you would care what kind of plant it was, as long as it was big enough and dense enough to hide you.

"Why is a globe so irresistible?" asked Mr. Port, the librarian. "Nobody can walk by it without giving it a twirl. It ought to be mounted on ball bearings."

"The world spins," Jude suggested. "It's more like the real thing if the globe does." He glanced over his shoulder. "—Mr. Port, I'm really in a big hurry."

"Perhaps I should hitch a motor to it and save the fingers of all my globe-twirlers." Mr. Port, unlike his mathematics colleague Mr. Evanson, was of the opinion that *subtle, indirect criticism* worked best with students. It didn't work very well, however, when the student was in such a hurry, so the real meaning of all this flew right past Jude.

"—Are you sure *this* is what you want?" Mr. Port, speaking of the yellow paperback, gave Jude a look first-grade teachers use when asking jumpy kids if they have to go to the bathroom. With his eyes on the bus Jude didn't notice.

"Yes," said Jude, "I want all three of them." He waved his hand over the pile without looking. Red, green, and yellow, what difference did it make? He wanted all three of them. "—I'm late for my bus or I'd take more time." He could see his bus was loaded. The back of it was inching forward out of the card catalogue window. The front half had disappeared.

Mr. Port wrinkled his brow, stamped the paperback, removed its signature card for Jude to sign, and pushed all three books across the desk to him.

"A year from now this will be much faster," he said. "We're going to put the whole library on a computer—you won't even have to sign for your books."

Mr. Port was also of the opinion that students should be kept informed and treated as equals. "If you don't have what you want here, come back tomorrow during study hall. I'll write you a pass in the morning. I'd like to see more

of you in this library, Jude, even if you are a globe-twirler."
Here was more subtle criticism, but also a pat on the back.
Mr. Port thought it was important to encourage good hab-
its.

"I'll be back," said Jude, racing away. "I've made up my
mind to read more. Thanks a lot, Mr. Port."

He tucked the books into a fold of a jacket he carried
over his arm and sprinted to the bus whose doors were now
closed. Phyllis Cobb, bus driver and his mother's best
friend, had released the parking brake and was coasting
forward with her foot on the clutch. Jude ran alongside
pounding on the door with his free hand till it popped open.

"Jude, you almost had to walk," said Phyllis, visibly relieved. "I'd about given up on you."

"I could hitchhike if I missed the bus."

"Your mom wouldn't think much of that. I wouldn't
even try it if I were you, not when you have old Phyllis to
get you home."

Old Phyllis was in her early forties, the same age as Kate
Henley. They had been classmates, here at Twin Rivers
High where Phyllis had won speech contests and graduated
first in her class. She had a tarnished trophy in a cabinet by
Principal Willoughby's office, a small replica of which she
kept polished in her china hutch at home.

Today and most days she drove her school bus, Phyllis
wore what she was wearing the August evening she and her
husband George had helped them move. The red baseball
cap, whose long bill formed an arch over her face, was the
same cap. She wore faded blue jeans, rolled up so their bot-
toms wouldn't flop around the clutch pedal, the same as in
August. Phyllis sat up straight with her bus driver's seat

cranked up as high as it would go. Alert as a bird, after quick glances to either side in her mirrors, she eased the orange hulk out into traffic.

Meanwhile, Mr. Port had joined the company of Miss Greshmer and Mr. Martin Evanson in the faculty lounge. Noting his arrival, Mr. Evanson had politely removed his hand from the art teacher's arm. Given the state of her acne especially, he did not wish to be suspected of flirting with Connie Greshmer. "How's it going for you today, Wally?" said Mr. Evanson.

Walter Port, librarian of Twin Rivers High, did not like to be called either of two things. He did not like to be referred to as a *media specialist*, and he did not like to be called *Wally*, a fact he had often tried to convey to Mr. Martin Evanson, using—of course—indirect, subtle criticism.

For example, once after being called Wally by Mr. Evanson, with Miss Greshmer as his witness, he had directed some remarks to the coffeepot on the counter behind them, explaining to the coffeepot how silly he thought this common habit of distorting perfectly good names to make them end with a *y* sound. So Cynthia became Cindy, Samuel became Sammy, and Constance became Connie. At this point Constance Greshmer blushed, though Mr. Port's gaze had stayed fixed upon the coffeepot. Then a further example of ruining a perfectly good name occurred to Mr. Port who promptly shared it with the coffeepot. "And Martin becomes *Martini*."

Behind him what had begun as Miss Greshmer's giggle became a coughing fit.

In his most serious geometer's tone, Mr. Evanson had said, "Actually, I think the name would be *Marty*." Casting aside any hint of acrimony, Mr. Evanson found all this much too philosophical. He might as well have been a coffeepot, so completely had the point of it escaped him. As far as he was concerned, the man who had just come in was *Wally*, Wally Port. And his opinion didn't change today when Mr. Port arrived.

"I've had a god-awful day, Wally, as I was just telling Connie here," said Mr. Evanson.

"Actually, I have only one complaint, *Martini* ..." said Mr. Port, refusing to elaborate.

7

Hide and Seek

Phyllis Cobb's bus had gotten no farther than the first school crossing where she waited for a line of elementary students to cross, all of them in Halloween costumes. At the head of the line was a fairy or perhaps a bird or butterfly. It had wings at any rate. In the middle came a pumpkin with black octopus arms. At the end of the line shambled unmistakably Frankenstein.

"I see you've got some books with you," she said to Jude.

"I went to the library—that's why I was late," said Jude.

As luck would have it, practically his only luck so far this day, he had been able to slide into a front seat immediately behind Phyllis and beside two jumpy first-graders, twins, one of them a cat for Halloween, the other a mouse. They both moved over, the cat nearly sitting on the mouse's lap, leaving more than half the seat to him. It seldom happened that big kids sat in the front of the bus. For Jude it was the best possible spot this afternoon, as far away as he could get from Peter Johnson and Ronny Faber.

"I like to see boys your age with books," Phyllis shouted over her shoulder so Jude could hear her above the general din—the window-rattling engine, the sixty voices behind them talking at once, the furtive tooting of a trumpet several rows back. "I don't like to see kids your age hitchhiking.

—Move along, Frankenstein, you won't scare anyone walking so slow. There are too many weird types in this world who might pick you up, Jude."

Jude cringed. He could never forgive Mandy Gordon for calling him that. He wound his jacket around the three books and stared at the back of Phyllis's head where innumerable tiny curls like blonde soap bubbles popped out from under her cap.

"I like books," Phyllis shouted. "I like novels mostly. What do you have there? Anything I've read?"

They had gotten as far as the first stoplight on their way out of Twin Rivers. Jude unwound his jacket and looked at the top book in his stack, the red one.

From somewhere behind him came a mournful bellow.

"—Hey, lay off that horn back there," Phyllis screamed spinning around too late to see a trumpet lowered behind a seat two rows from the back.

After two more short toots, like hiccups, the trumpet gave up. "*Washington at Valley Forge*," Jude read from the book spine, his first look at it.

The mouse and the cat giggled.

"What's so funny?" asked Jude. The mouse and the cat were silent.

Then Phyllis said the one thing people always say about George Washington, not that he's on the quarter; not that he's on the dollar bill; not that they named a state, the capital of the whole country, and a third of the schools in America after him. "He never told a lie," said Phyllis.

Beneath her gaze at the stoplight an old woman tottered through the crosswalk pulling a wire shopping cart behind her. A celery top stuck out from a sack within it. The light flashed green.

"Step along now, Granny," said Phyllis under her breath. "I always try to be patient with old people," she shouted back to Jude. "We'll be old someday." This afternoon Phyllis felt brimming with quaint advice: Read books ... never lie ... be kind to old folks ... don't let weirdoes pick you up.

It all made some kind of sense to Jude—at least he wouldn't have argued with any of it—but the trouble was that it didn't make very valuable sense as far as he could see. It didn't answer the questions he most needed to answer. It didn't solve any problems for him.

What should I do about Jeannie T? he wanted to ask. *Why do I feel the need to defend her, even if I make a fool of myself? What should I do with this awful job Harmon Grove loaded on me? How do you keep from being weird? Tell me that, Phyllis, if you can.*

If he had really asked Phyllis such questions, she would have provided answers. Phyllis always had answers, but Jude hadn't always had secrets. He wasn't as used to secrets as Phyllis was to having answers, and more than needing her answers, at this point, he needed to keep his secrets. He hadn't learned much about triangles in geometry class today, but he had learned no good would come of talking about Jeannie T. Why else was he forced to sing in front of his class, and now why was he sitting with first-graders? It all came from revealing things.

The steel bus floor throbbed beneath Jude's feet. His head throbbed for other reasons. He was afraid to turn around. He was sure that everyone behind him was looking at the back of his head and laughing. They were elbowing their neighbors and pointing at him, while he kept his eyes fixed straight ahead on Phyllis's bubbly hair and the old lady with her celery stalk who by making them wait was only prolonging his agony.

Behind where Jude dared not look, several carloads of Twin Rivers High students were also made to wait. Mufflers popped. Radios blared from open windows. Somebody's bass woofers boomed as shouts flew between sidewalk and street, between car and car. The senior class was on parade, waving to itself, lighting cigarettes. Girls took dramatically long puffs. Boys took short ones and looked at the girls. The senior class thought very fondly of itself, whooping its importance, while in the face of all this, stopping most of it in its tracks, the old woman towed her celery home without looking up or taking the least notice. The senior class, for all she seemed to care, was a flock of blackbirds. Jude's orange bus was a pumpkin pile. Had he been less upset, Jude might have discovered a lesson in this.

"At last!" said Phyllis. She eased her pumpkin pile into the crossing and out onto the main street through Twin Rivers. "What else have you got there, Jude? Any novels?" asked Phyllis minutes later as they waited at yet another signal light.

Jude lifted the red book to glance at the green. It was called *Robinson Crusoe*. He shouted this at the back of Phyllis's head. "Is that a novel?"

"It's a story about a shipwrecked man surviving alone on an island in the ocean. It's a good book for you, living out in the park like you do—stick with it, even if you find it pretty tough reading in places." Phyllis always had answers, advice and answers.

As for Jude, the thought of living alone on an island seemed especially appealing this afternoon, and now that they were moving, heading for home, he was beginning to feel better. In a way, he'd been shipwrecked in geometry class this afternoon, but at least he was already familiar with his island. For once Hawkers Park and the Perch sounded good to him. He thought it really quite amazing, his luck in grabbing just the books he needed at this moment in his life. Perhaps it was true that everyone had a guardian angel or some sort of good fairy looking after them. It was either a guardian angel or just blind luck to have grabbed without looking both honest George Washington and now some guy named Robinson who had an island all to himself.

Five minutes later they were already on the outskirts of Twin Rivers which, though it was the biggest town in the area, wasn't very big all the same. Along their route ahead lay the muted, mid-autumn scenery of farms, lakes, and forests between Twin Rivers and Hawkers Park, a country which not even the ruddy sunlight of this *Indian Summer* day could make to seem very exciting, with most of its leaves fallen and its fields brown from a half-dozen frosts.

Today for a change Jude found it enticing, and the farther into it they drove, the better he felt. Twice on small bridges they crossed the North Crow on its southward course winding through meadow marshes where here and there a few milk cows would be grazing on the higher ground nosing through dead pasture grasses. With kids getting off and a line of cars strung out behind them hanging back and passing when they found an opening, the bus emptied and quieted by the mile. Gone the trumpet player to a yard with a barking lab and an old barn leaning toward a topless windmill. Gone the giggly girls sitting behind Jude. Gone the mouse and the cat to a trailer house on the edge of a pine forest.

And gone for the time being all talk from Phyllis, as she concentrated on her flashing lights, mirrors, and the stop sign she extended every time she dropped off riders. All this caution had earned her safety awards year after year, the pins of which she wore on her cap.

Jude sometimes went with his mother to Phyllis's split-level brick home in the lake country several miles north of Hawkers Park. Since she and her husband George had no children and no other guests that Jude ever met or heard of, their home with its vaulted wood ceilings, three bathrooms, and fireplaces downstairs and up seemed pointlessly big, as quiet and empty as a church between services. It filled him with yawns and whispers and fidgets he never felt elsewhere.

While Phyllis and his mother talked the hours away, usually in the kitchen near a coffeepot, he had to keep moving or risk falling asleep. So he would wander all over the place, past bedrooms whose pillows were always plumped and curtains always drawn as if never an eye wanted sunshine there, never a head took its rest.

In the living room, plants hung limp as leftover salads. Even the aquarium fish seemed sleepy in their ribbons of bubbles. The recreation room downstairs might have been built for him alone. Its pool table balls never moved between his visits. The yellow and green he had shot into a side pocket were there when he came back. The balls he racked were still in the rack. If he left the red ball and the black eight lying on top, they'd be there still, glued to the spots where his last shot sent them. He might have stepped out a minute ago to go to the bathroom or get a can of coke, or he might have been gone for six weeks—it was the same either way. Nothing changed, and the balls made melancholy clunks when he shot them around, as if from sheer boredom all their wooden hearts had grown hollow.

Whatever life could be found in her huge house came from Phyllis. She chattered like a plump talking bird fluttering through it, throwing open her refrigerator and cupboard doors, inviting you to take whatever you wanted to eat and drink, and sit down anywhere with it. Phyllis liked reading as much as her husband didn't. She discussed novels with her good friend Kate Henley, never with George who was both suspicious of books and his wife's reading them. Whenever he was near enough to overhear, Kate—fearing trouble—changed the subject to the weather or Phyllis's garden, or she would ask about George's mother. George wasn't necessarily ready to talk about these subjects either, but anything was better than books.

Phyllis could take you into her pantry, a place George never went, and show you her paperbacks on shelves with canned peas and snap beans for bookends. Jars of spiced crabapples she canned last summer divided the classics from recent bestsellers. "My library," she would say, not sadly but with chirpy satisfaction as if she liked it that way.

"I just hate to throw them away when I'm done reading them, but even the sight of a book puts George in a tizzy."

George owned a construction company whose dump trucks and bulldozers, when they weren't out on a job, were parked in open sheds across a field from their house. He was a sandy-haired, moody sort who had the habit of rubbing his nose when he talked, which as a rule wasn't often, but became an avalanche of talk whenever it did come. Ordinarily, he parceled out his words like a card player dealing from a slippery deck. Upset him, though, and he would fling the whole deck at once.

Jude was thinking about all this and doing his best not to think about geometry class and Peter and Ronny sitting behind him as his bus emptied and drew nearer to Hawkers Park where he would be let off at the junction of the highway and the sandy road. He stood up from his seat the moment he could see the sandy road a hundred yards ahead.

"You're supposed to stay seated until we stop," said Phyllis glancing back as she switched on the bus's flashing red lights.

Jude sat down again on the edge of the seat with his feet pointed toward the door which for him had become an escape hatch.

He had made up his mind to quit spying on Jeannie T. Phyllis's novels hidden away in her pantry led him to this decision. It seemed like the only way for him to become normal again. In his free time after school and on weekends, he planned to read books instead of roaming around the park alone with too many thoughts running through his head. If Jeannie T didn't skip out, Harmon Grove would never know that he hadn't done his spying. He was aware of weaknesses in his reasoning, but he ignored them for the time being.

Like Phyllis he had things to hide—for the first time in his life—and it seemed to him that the more he tried to free himself from them, the more he had to hide. It began when he had to hide from Jeannie T as he spied on her behind her cabin. Then he had to hide Jeannie T's old songs so they wouldn't slip out and make a fool of him again in front of his classmates. Now, he couldn't possibly tell his mother what had happened in school today. All these concealed things would grow like the hidden piles of novels Phyllis Cobb read. He wondered if they affected her the way those songs affected him. Did they pop out sometimes, revealing themselves, as she chattered away with George in the room? In spite of her careful hiding, did he recognize in her, as Jude's classmates did in him, the things she had by heart?

Everything hidden led to something else you had to hide. After a while not even a large pantry could contain it all.

8

You Can't Win

Peter and Ronny were the last ones on the bus when Jude got off where the highway met the sandy road. They lived on neighboring farms on the very edge of the school district only a mile or so from Hawkers Park and as far as Jude was concerned, suddenly much too close for his comfort.

"Be sure to read *Robinson Crusoe*," Phyllis sang out as double doors snapped open and Jude fled. "Say hi to your mom for me."

"See you," said Jude.

Doing his best to appear nonchalant, he walked out across the highway with Phyllis's red lights flashing above him. His books were under his arm with his jacket wrapped around them. Phyllis's questions had not quite gotten to the bottom of his pile.

Straight ahead was the sandy road. Nearby on that side were a gas station and a roadside café. Across the highway a hundred feet or so ahead stood a small, white frame church, two white frame houses, a picnic area, and a trailer house. All this on both sides was called Twisters. Not that it was considered a town. It didn't have a post office, a mayor, its name on a map, or even a highway sign identifying it. People called it Twisters from a time twenty years ago when a tornado roared through and blew most of it away.

Peter Johnson slid open a bus window in back.

"Hey, Jude baby, sing to us!" he screeched as the bus accelerated. "Sing!"

His voice ought to have shrunk and lost its edge as the distance between him and Jude increased, but to Jude it became yet more piercing. It stabbed right through him puncturing and releasing the better feelings slowly building within him on the ride home. He was flung back to being weird.

Phyllis shifted into second across from the picnic area. Several cars were passing her at once with Peter's head out the window looking back at Jude over the tops of them. His long red hair blew into his face so that it looked more like the back of his head than the front. Phyllis reeled around to shout at him. The bus swerved, her safety record teetered, a passing car honked and sped by. Peter drew his head inside and closed the window.

"I ought to haul you back to Twin Rivers and make you walk the whole way home," she shouted.

"I could hitchhike," Peter said.

Phyllis wished he would. She wished somebody weird would offer him a ride.

Ahead of Jude on the way down to Hawkers Park from Twisters the shadows of a fence row of burr oaks in low sunlight lay like piano keys across the sandy road, sharps and flats only. He had begun down the road when suddenly and with conviction he turned back toward the highway. His free hand groped for two quarters in his pants pocket.

Inside Twisters Café, empty except for its owner, a skinny man sitting on a high stool behind the lunch counter, Jude slid his quarters into a pinball machine called

Wild Card. It sputtered and pulsed to life in a blaze of colors chasing each other, winking the whole deck of cards at him, the joker among them, most of all the joker, it seemed.

Dismayed to discover that he had an audience, Jude took a deep breath and tensed as he played his first chrome ball. It rolled through a gate, caromed diagonally between pairs of flashing bumpers, dropped through a chute where the Jack of Hearts stood, giving him a hundred points, and instantly plummeted toward him. Jude danced on his tiptoes. Though the action lay entirely with his fingers, his whole body swayed into the machine moving it ever so slightly as he worked its two sets of flippers. The ball fell between and was lost. *GAME OVER* flashed out one letter at a time on a hand of eight playing cards, and then all at once. He had tilted *Wild Card* on his first ball. Behind him the skinny man laughed.

"You can't win that way," he chortled. "You've got to have a real soft touch with that machine. She's as temperamental as a woman, if you know what I mean." He winked when he said this.

Jude slid his books off the lunch counter.

"Aren't you going to give her another try?" the skinny man asked over the brim of a white coffee mug he raised to his lips.

"Nope, I've got to get home." Instead of meeting the skinny man's gaze, he focused on his white apron, its soup stain to the left, its coffee to the right, its hamburger grease all over.

"You can't win if you don't practice either. It takes practice and a real soft touch, same with a girlfriend."

He reached under his apron, under the hamburger grease stains, and pulled out two quarters which he slid across the counter to Jude. While he was talking, between sips of coffee, he rolled around in his mouth a wad of gum or tobacco. "I was noticing the names of those books you've got there, and I sure get a bang out of that top one. When's it due anyway?" His nostrils dilated as he grinned.

"In two weeks, I guess," Jude answered, backing toward the door. He wondered why anyone other than Mr. Port would care when his library books were due.

"I never would have guessed it from the look of you," said the skinny man. His eyes twinkled. He drowned his laughter in sips of coffee.

Jude shrugged and stepped back outside into an autumn whose orange light burnished the frame buildings across the highway, making them seem built of metal and stone rather than painted cedar and pine. A bell over the door rang as he left the café. He hadn't noticed it coming in.

He was so unhappy with himself today, he could agree with the skinny man whose quarters he'd left where they lay. He was sure he wouldn't win much of anything, *ever*, the way he was going. He had wasted his money on a pinball machine he didn't feel like playing, trying to prove something to himself and most of all to Peter Johnson, who was probably home by now, eating a peanut butter sandwich or a banana, and not caring at all where Jude was or whether he could do things as normal as playing pinball.

Trying to escape being weird was like trying to swim when you didn't know anything about it. The more you splashed and kicked around, the sooner you sank to the bottom and swallowed half the pool before you got your head out again. So he felt even less normal for having tried so hard. With Halloween day on the brink of becoming Halloween, he'd become, even without a mask and costume, just the sort of odd creature you'd expect to see walking down a darkening road, this night in particular.

He didn't see how he could feel any worse—then he glanced for the first time at the last of his three library books. The yellow book having begun the trip home on the bottom of his stack now lay on top. He groaned and slapped his forehead with his hand. Now he understood why Mr. Port had asked him in particular if he was sure he wanted that one, and why the skinny man had asked when it was due. His words and sniffing, sneering laughter pursued him down the sandy road, burning in his ears. The yellow book had been re-bound, as library paperbacks sometimes are, and painted on its spine and front cover was The *Joys of Motherhood* for the whole world to see and laugh at. He felt like the weirdest person who ever lived.

Had he carried matches or a lighter and smoked like the Twin Rivers seniors, he might have burnt *The Joys of Motherhood* then and there. This was his first thought. His second concerned the good chance that only Mr. Port and the skinny man knew about it. He hid it in the mailbox at the end of Harmon Grove's driveway, certain that nobody was likely to look there. One of these days he would take it out and smuggle it back to the library. *One of these days.*

One of these days would have to be better than this day, this awful day of tricks without treats. His heart had sunk with the sun by the time he reached their cabin yard, and standing there at the end of its driveway, he looked back up the sandy road and imagined his way over a few little hills and around a bend or two through the woods to where the highway waited to lead him tomorrow back into a world he would have to face again. Would this hiding ever end? Whether he actually spoke these words or simply thought them he couldn't have said. Either way, they seemed to echo in his heart and in a world where his heart no longer fit.

9

Tricks Without Treats

At home finally, Jude went out Halloween evening before supper and pretended to be checking on Jeannie T. Instead of walking up to the Woodcock, he sat on the Rabbit's stoop, the eleventh cabin in the row, and watched stars come out. By the time it was dark enough to see every star he would be able to see, he still hadn't found a solution.

The road back to normal had to begin somewhere. He wondered whether it would help if he quit spying. All along he felt it was wrong, and his problems in school today seemed a reminder that nothing is weirder than to keep on doing something when you feel you shouldn't. So instead, what if he read books in any spare time he had and stayed away from the far end of the park?

No sooner than had he asked himself, he realized it would never work. This plan was like a mask put on for Halloween. It didn't change the face beneath it, nor would it change the face of things outside: The singer still might run away if she fell behind with her rent, and his mother still would be blamed if they failed to catch her doing it. That failure might be his fault, and his alone, but his mother would bear the blame if he didn't do his job. They were still Harmon Grove's caretakers. For half their rent, they were expected to help him bully someone who was just as poor as they were, and maybe even having a harder time of it. An owl hooting somewhere in the distant ravine seemed to agree.

He had to be the spy. There was no way out of it, and no way back to normal. These were facts no decision of his would change, and no humiliation at school could make him ignore. He might stay away from the Woodcock today, but he would have to go back tomorrow afternoon. He would always have to go back. He walked home to the Perch and hid himself in his remaining library books.

He started reading *Robinson Crusoe*, as a full moon rose above an approaching cloud bank, and then climbed behind the bare branches of the park trees before dissolving into a glowing spot when clouds caught up with it. Phyllis Cobb was right about *Robinson Crusoe*: it was a hard book from the first, and he spent an hour with it without even getting to the shipwreck, let alone an island. Robinson was arguing with a father whose advice he wanted to ignore. Jude thought this interesting.

He was sitting in the living room end of the room the Henleys had begun calling their *mansion*. They didn't know how else to describe it, since it was their kitchen on the other end, a dining room in between, and at various times Jude's bedroom, an office, a study, and served the purposes of other rooms you might find in a mansion. Here on the living room end were a couch and a stuffed chair with no more shape and perhaps less support than the lap of a very fat person.

With its exhausted springs complaining every time he shifted position, the harder *Robinson Crusoe* got, the more the chair complained about it. Since he slept on the couch, and at other times had enough of its own melancholy sagging and complaining, he seldom sat there. Both pieces had come with the cabin, belonged to Harmon Grove, and seemed to share his instinctive annoyance with punks, an annoyance that also possessed the tottering, enfeebled floor lamp by which Jude read, for if it didn't wobble of its own will, it certainly wobbled of Harmon's, twitching its light over the pages of *Robinson Crusoe* till he grew dizzy.

"Hey, it's Halloween, isn't it?" Kate Henley asked as if she just that moment thought of it, which was not quite the case, since she had been expecting Jude to mention it before this.

She glanced up from the kitchen table where she sat working. She looked right at her son, this not being one of her times for looking far off. She'd been addressing bulletins and advertising circulars for a small tool company in Twin Rivers, an old-fashioned enterprise that liked its business to project the personal touch, no computers, no automatic addressing machines, only a Kate to address each piece by hand, to stuff and lick each envelope. She made five cents each. After a month's experience, she could do a hundred an hour, but each evening's work was never more than an hour, sometimes less.

"It's the end of the month already—I always address Texas at the end of the month."

Texas was much less, only fifty or so, from Amarillo, through El Paso, to a place called Yellow Sky. This might have required no more than half an hour, but she had taken her time this evening, and was still in the middle somewhere the other side of Fort Worth.

Sometimes Jude helped her lick envelopes until both their tongues became so dry that they wanted to laugh but couldn't, and when they tried talking to each other, they could only make funny sounds. "We're partners in adversity," Kate might say to her son at times like that.

"Do you have much to do tonight, Mom?" he asked.

"Not really, Texas is about half done, and then there's a few for Washington, Wyoming, and the others—you know how it is on this end of the alphabet. What are you doing sitting around home on Halloween?"

Jude shrugged. "I'll lick Texas for you," he said, reaching for Amarillo, suppressing a yawn, and too willingly setting aside

Robinson Crusoe on a table which otherwise *Washington at Valley Forge* shared with a pack of cigarettes and the Twin Rivers weekly shopper. He licked Amarillo, Austin, and Dallas. The glue on the envelope flaps had a faint peppermint taste.

This was the most recent of odd jobs his mother held while he grew up. Some of them had been much odder jobs. When they lived in Twin Rivers, she had sold garden seed and women's handbags door-to-door. Walking home from school to his grandmother's house or to the apartment over the hardware store or to wherever they were living at the time, he occasionally caught a glimpse of her standing on a doorstep or crossing a street with eight purses on each arm. He would have run to join her, but she never wanted him along when she was selling.

"I don't want people to think that I have you tag along to fish for sympathy," she once admonished him when he had run two blocks to catch up with her. That day she was towing a red coaster wagon loaded with seed and flowering plants in peat moss. "I'm selling marigolds and petunias, not my situation," she said, but this one afternoon he was allowed to walk with her for a time.

Another year she became the local sales representative for *The Family Disease Home Medical Bible*, an impressive volume fat as the real bible and resembling it with its gilded page ends and bound-in satin markers. It had fold- out colored pictures of the large intestine, the pancreas, the heart, even the muscles used to wiggle the big toe. The pancreas was orange, and the large intestine purple enough to make you gag. Its blue heart never made you think of a valentine. Jude would never forget the heart. He never could pass by that book without peaking at it. So substantial it seemed, so shiny with life, so determined to beat that it almost throbbed there in front of him. Somewhere in the book's glossary was the name of the disease that had stilled his father's heart—the unpronounceable name—and a short paragraph explaining it was so uncommon that this book, large as it was, would ignore it otherwise.

Peddled door-to-door this book accounted for both the dog bite scars on his mother's ankles. Dogs seemed to hate *The Family Disease Home Medical Bible,* objecting to its rabies section perhaps, where they along with skunks came in for a lot of criticism. Kate had a third dog bite scar, on her right hand between her forefinger and thumb, the work of a poodle Phyllis Cobb owned and George Cobb drowned immediately afterwards in a burlap sack in the North Crow.

Jude licked Galveston and Houston. He thought about the fight he'd witnessed between George and Phyllis the same afternoon when George returned from the river, she screaming that the poodle should have been checked for rabies, George screaming back that the only disease it had was a mental problem, Kate with her bandaged hand trying to calm them both. "George," said Phyllis, "You're the one with the mental problem!"

Jude licked some small Texas towns.

But George Cobb—to give him credit—went back to the river, which was shallow in that dry season, and waded around and dove for an hour till he came up with the poodle in the weighted burlap sack, and then he took it to a veterinarian who soon notified Kate she needn't take the series of rabies shots.

"You're working fast tonight," Jude's mother noticed. "Tongue nice and wet?"

"Mmm," said Jude.

"Aren't you going out trick-or-treating, Jude?"

He sucked in his cheeks, cleared his mind of Phyllis and George, and squeezed out enough saliva to say that he wasn't going anywhere. He thought it silly of big kids to threaten people for candy, even if the threats were only make-believe.

"You're getting big, Jude—you're growing up," she said almost wistfully, and into her eyes came that faraway look as if she imagined a time not far off when he would leave home, and she'd be sitting someplace like this without him.

"That's just it," Jude said. "I'm too old for Halloween now, and anyway it's too far." He was thinking of the few houses at Twisters where he might have gone, in one of which lived the skinny man, another reason for staying home tonight.

Kate wrote addresses without looking up again, her pen gliding easily over the envelopes though she held it so tightly that the veins of her small hand bulged, and the scar of the poodle's bite, which was normally red, turned white.

"If you think Twisters is too far, then for sure you must be too old," she said. "It would be too far for me, but you walk up there every morning to catch your bus. You walk home from there every afternoon."

"I do walk a lot—that's a good point. I've already made the trip twice today. You don't mind if I stay home, do you?"

Jude didn't want to see the skinny man again today, not for a case of candy bars. Still it might have been simpler just to go through the motions as he had when pretending to check on Miss Thorpe. He might walk to Twisters and pretend to pass from door-to-door, return empty-handed, and say nobody was home.

"Of course I don't mind if you stay home. You can take charge of things here if anyone comes to the door. And I'm glad to have you licking Texas for me. Turn on the outside light when you're done. There are two bags of candy in the cupboard."

"Candy," said Jude, all at once overcome with gloom, "candy is nothing to me these days."

"Jude, I think you must be in love."

He squirmed in his chair. He licked San Antonio, almost the last of tongue-parching Texas. He stood up and peered out a window in the cabin before turning on the light. "Nobody will come," he said. "This park is like another planet this time of year." For the moment, he wasn't entirely unhappy with this thought.

"Oh come on, Jude," she gently scolded. "It's not that bad—it's pleasant enough, it's quiet, it's home.

"I wasn't thinking it was bad."

"Then are you sure you're not in love?"

"Mom!" He wheeled around defiantly. There she sat, as quiet as this park, as pleasant as its summers, braver than Washington at Valley Forge or anyone he could ever read about in books. Toward her he could never be angry.

He turned to the window again, and as he did so, he thought he saw something like a white ribbon floating down across it. He heard a scratching sound. Across the way, Harmon's Grove's cabin was dark. In one of its windows Jude could see reflected a shaft of moonlight flashing between clouds. When he flipped on the light outside over their door, shadows leaped out between their cabin and Harmon's. He turned away and sank once more into the shapeless chair. He heard more scratching sounds.

"Not everybody is as old as you are," she said with a laugh, "and some that *are* might not feel as old. They might not think it's too far to come here."

He could have reminded her no kids lived at Twisters, and that it was too far from anywhere else to here. Who would leave Twin Rivers with its hundreds of houses to look for candy here where there were but twelve cabins, ten of them empty? Instead of saying any of this, he leaned to pick up *Robinson Crusoe* on the coffee table. The chair sank as he reached out, and either from that or the depth of his gloom he was nearly pitched onto the floor.

His mother's optimism, however, couldn't be restrained. "Maybe the Johnson and Faber boys will stop by— what are their names?"

"Peter and Ronny," he nearly groaned. This suggestion, he knew, was meant to cheer him, but just as in the case of his own attempts to be normal, the harder she tried, the worse he felt. "They'll go to Twin Rivers if they go any-where." Oh, did Jude hope they wouldn't come here! All he needed was to hear once more today Peter screaming, "Sing, baby, sing!" All he needed was to try explaining *that* to his mother.

"There, I've finished Washington and the Virginias," she said. "I'm done." She licked the last few envelope flaps and put the end of the alphabet in a shopping bag on the floor where everything else had already gone.

Meanwhile Jude skipped ahead to Robinson's island, not reading so much as glancing at words, and between times thinking he heard more sounds outside.

"Mom, did you hear that?" "What, Jude?"

"It sounds like an animal or something scratching on our wall." Kate, who hadn't heard anything, thought it might have been wind blowing through shrubbery growing close to one wall of the Perch or perhaps a mouse in the wall or her son's imagination. After all it was Halloween they had been discussing. Wasn't the night supposed to be spooky?

"I did hear something from Harmon Grove though." She pulled a letter folded in two from the pocket of her blue car-digan. "He's getting along fine in Florida, it seems."

"You mean the guy even knows how to write?"

"Of course he does, and actually his penmanship is pretty good. He says it's eighty degrees there, and he was asked to referee at a professional wrestling match. He says it rains every afternoon at three o'clock where he lives, and then the sun comes out again." She paused and wondered if she should reveal that Miss Thorpe was already a month behind with her rent, that Harmon wanted to know if he'd been checking on her.

"She practices her songs every afternoon," Jude said when she told him at last. "It's like listening to something on the radio—if you're there every afternoon between four and five, you hear the same program."

"Just like the rain in Florida where Harmon lives."

Jude was reminded of George Washington who Phyllis said never told lies. George seemed to reproach him from his closed book on the coffee table. He had to tell her the truth.

"I didn't go all the way up there today, but Miss Thorpe was home yesterday, and ... I'll check again tomorrow if you want me to." Neither reading nor even standing on his head would give him a way out of this, especially when she was already behind with her rent. There was no way to stop being weird. He would just have to go through it, all the way through until he got to the other end, wherever that was and whatever it made of him.

"Would you check, please? I hate it, spying on her like this, but would you go up there for sure, so I can write Harmon and tell him everything's all right?"

Jude was stuck. He closed *Robinson Crusoe* and stared at its green cover.

"Jude, can you think of anything else I should tell him when I write?"

He bounded up from the shapeless chair and sank down again till only the floor could have stopped him. "Tell him how much I like this chair," he said. "Tell him how much it reminds me of him."

She stood up from the table and came across the room to sit near him. "It is really a wreck," she agreed. "He told me that he'd bring us a better one from one of the other cabins, but he never got around to it or it just slipped his mind, I guess."

Harmon's floor lamp had wobbled her way when she sat down. His couch springs moaned, though she was no heavier than Jude, and though she sat down lightly with one leg doubled under her as if she meant to get right up again.

"I'm sorry to bother you when you're reading," she went on. "I'm afraid that we've gotten ourselves into a mess with this Miss Thorpe affair. It helps pay our rent, but I don't like it, and I can see that you don't."

"I don't mind so much," Jude said without conviction. "We'll get by." Conviction this time—they always got by somehow.

"Do you really feel that way?" She doubted that he did.

"About getting by, yes ... but to tell the truth, I don't like spying on Miss Thorpe. I feel sorry for her—she's alone like us. I've heard her sing those old songs so many times that they stick in my head."

"We're not alone, Jude. We have friends, and you don't really know about Miss Thorpe—unless you've discovered things you're not telling me—so you can't be sure what her real situation is, or how you should feel about her. She might have lots of friends." She leaned toward him over the couch arm. "Imagination—it might all be your imagination." She brushed from her face a strand of brown hair that had strayed there.

Jude noticed a trace of gray in it, *not* something he imagined.

The floor lamp wobbled his way, its light dancing over the cover of *Robinson Crusoe* lying closed on his lap. Lights were off in the kitchen end of their main room. A slash of illumination from the light over their door sliced through a gap between the door window curtains and cut across the yellow table precisely where his mother had been addressing envelopes. Harmon's letter lay in the center of it as if in a spotlight. Projected from somewhere through one of the windows, either from the moon reappearing in a sky grown cloudless again or from the light over their door, a shadow flitted across a wall. As he met his mother's gaze, Jude had barely a glimpse of it.

"I know how you feel," she was saying, "but Harmon also has his rights. He can't have people living free in his cabins. Can you see his side of it?" She stammered then, as she often did when she was unsure of herself.

Jude nodded because he felt that's what she wanted from him, but he couldn't see Harmon Grove's viewpoint at all. Without Miss Thorpe to live there, his Woodcock cabin would be empty for the off-season anyway. Without her, he wouldn't get any money at all for it.

The same held true for them in the Perch, but if Kate realized this, she let it pass without saying so. "I know you don't mean it, Jude—I can tell by the look in your eyes. You can't see things Harmon's way because your sense of justice gets in the way."

"If you mean that I don't think it's fair ..."

"It's the world that so often isn't fair—that's what you're discovering now. It's about more than Harmon and Miss

Thorpe ..." She paused and wondered if this was the time to reveal some news she had, a complete change of subject. "— Hey, though, you know what? Phyllis Cobb thinks that I could have a job driving a school bus this winter. What do you think of that? All I need do is pass a test for the special license. With a job like that, we could move out of here when Harmon comes back from Florida."

"School buses are noisy," Jude said. "People honk their horns at you sometimes, and they shake their fists. Little kids throw up on the floor. I'd rather hitchhike than ride a school bus. I'd rather spy on Miss Thorpe than see you drive one."

"Jude, you *are* a wet blanket tonight! It's your sense of justice again. Phyllis doesn't mind the job—she likes it. You're so like your father, wanting to protect the people you care for. That was the hardest part of dying for him. It wasn't what was happening to him but knowing he couldn't protect people any longer. *Protective*, Jude, that's what you are, like your father, and a grouchy wet blanket tonight." She playfully poked him on the shoulder. The floor lamp wobbled. "Did something go wrong at school today?"

Jude swallowed hard and said, "No." He had never seen such a day for having to hide things.

When his mother talked about his feelings, he felt embarrassed. When she talked about his father, that was something else. Much harder to say what he felt then. She might have been talking about fairies or guardian angels. It might have been Santa Claus or the Easter Bunny or a shadow you might have seen and couldn't explain, so you thought it was just your imagination playing tricks on you. Had there really been such a creature as *your father*?

But it was true that he wanted to protect her—wherever that came from in him—and he wanted to protect people like Miss Thorpe from the likes of Harmon Grove. If that was what it meant to have a *sense of justice*, then he had one for sure, no denying it. Strange, though, when you're a kid, everything you are you seem to have gotten from somebody else, from grandparents, a distant uncle, your mother, a father you never knew. People talked about you that way, as if nothing you *were* simply came from you, and nobody had to look any further to explain it.

"I'll let you get back to your reading. What is it?"

When he showed her the book, she stood up and walked to the window looking out over the park from their kitchen sink. She didn't want him to see her tears, two of them, one glistening with sudden joy and surprise, the other with an old sadness.

"Your father read that! We were dating, and sometimes we would meet after school in the Twin Rivers Public Library. He had graduated the year before and then lost his job over the winter, so some afternoons he spent in the library reading and waiting for me to show up...."

She hesitated, not because she was unable to recall these details, but because she thought of them so often without speaking of them. When she resumed, her stammer was there along with it.

"One afternoon—it must have been nearly Easter, just before he found work again and we couldn't meet there any more—I found him reading *Robinson Crusoe* in the library. Oh, Jude, your father was such a smart man. He worked with his hands, but when he read things, he could take them to heart and make them his own. How his eyes would glow. I remember his excitement over that book, and as he walked me home to Grandma's house, he read to me some passages that he especially liked; nearly walked into a lamp post with his nose in that book. See! I said you are like him—you even read the same books!"

She said all this, with her back to him yet, still gazing out the window, for the moment seeing nothing out there except a distant past.

Jude wasn't such a wet blanket nor had he the heart to explain it was all a coincidence, and that he'd taken this book out of the school library without glancing at its title, with no more thought about it than he'd given *The Joys of Motherhood*, which he was quite sure his father had never read.

And his father? He couldn't for the life of him imagine the man. He wanted to, but he couldn't. When he forced his imagination to picture his parents walking home from the public library that afternoon long ago, all he could see was his mother walking alone, the way she had always been, the way she was now looking outside with her back to him. *Alone, though this time not quite alone, for something else was there.*

He bolted for the door. "Jude, what is it?"

"Out there! Mom, don't you see it?"

Because Kate's thoughts and eyes had been elsewhere, she hadn't noticed what looked like white tape stretched across the upper portion of their kitchen window above her head. Their screen door screeched as usual, but along with this came a snapping sound of something stretching and breaking as Jude thrust it open and leaped outside.

By the time his mother had gotten that far, he was already on the sandy road running toward Twisters. She called after him. In the moonlit distance ahead of him he could discern two figures on bicycles drawing away, the red reflectors on their bike pedals seeming to blink as they went around and caught moonlight slanting through the roadside trees. He knew he had no hope of catching up. He also knew who he was chasing, no mistaking it. He shouted, and answering back came laughter as Peter and Ronny reached the highway, and their bicycles flew out of sight around a corner.

Perhaps because he had run so fast and so far and shouted after them, and perhaps because they had fled like cowards when they knew he was chasing them, Jude felt better than he had all day as he made his way back down the sandy road to the end of the driveway where his mother stood.

"You were right, Mom, when you said, 'We're not alone here.' And you were also right about Peter and Ronny maybe showing up."

"That was them?"

Jude nodded. He had in hand several feet of the paper streamer they had wrapped across their screen door and entirely around the Perch. As they walked back to their cabin, he crumpled it up in a ball so that his mother couldn't see what was written on it. While she waited at the door, he walked around the cabin pulling it off windows and walls where it had been taped. He rolled it up carefully so that anything written there would also be hidden from view, and compressing it into a tight roll, he slid it into his jacket pocket hanging on a hook beside the door.

"Well, I guess it wouldn't be Halloween without at least one trick," Kate said not quite bravely, for while she didn't mind a couple of young pranksters in the dark outside their cabin, the fact that they had managed to be there, doing what they did almost unnoticed, reminded her of how isolated they were in the park this time of year, and how helpless, without even a phone. She shivered. "I really wish Harmon had put Miss Thorpe down here in the next cabin," she said. "We'd all feel better about it."

Meantime Jude's thoughts were elsewhere. He paced through their mansion for a few minutes, pausing sometimes to glance out windows, as if to assure himself that Peter and Ronny weren't back. Once when passing the sagging couch, he picked up a cushion and gave it a punch.

Kate lay down in her bedroom awhile. Jude at last tore open one of the candy bags and ate a handful of orange jack-o-lanterns. He laid aside *Robinson Crusoe*, which had grown all the more impenetrable on account of his father's interest in it. He picked up *Washington at Valley Forge*, the first sentence of which caught his eye and stayed at hand the rest of the evening. *For Washington and his troops winter at Valley Forge was a lonely and dispiriting time.*

Ten o'clock. The moon had long since risen above their kitchen window, out of sight over a gable. A potted fern hanging there was merely a silhouette again.

"Happy Halloween," Kate said. She stood before him in a blue terry robe with steaming cups of cider in her hands.

"Happy Halloween, I guess," he said taking his cup and raising it to hers till they clinked together.

"No guessing about it, Jude. Happy for sure, even a funny trick to laugh about. —Now I see you're with General Washington. What does he have to say this evening?"

"He had a bad winter," Jude said.

"Well, I suppose he didn't mind it so much when the war was over, and he'd become President—it must have been a good story to tell his grandchildren."

After they had drunk, she turned off the outside light, set the door's dead bolt lock, and brought out from her bedroom a pillow and blankets for Jude's bed on the couch. He spread out the blankets and tucked one end under the cushions. With the wobbly lamp extinguished but still wobbling, he lay down in darkness no darker than gray because all the Perch's windows glowed now with the light of the full moon high up over its roof.

His mother spoke to him from the gray darkness of her room. "Jude, do you remember when you were a little boy, how on Halloween we'd cut jack-o-lantern faces out of grocery sacks and tape them behind our window shades? With the lights on inside, they glowed through the windows as orange as real pumpkins. We always wondered what people thought of them, whether they were frightening. If nobody stops by to tell you, you never find out, do you?"

"Maybe I should have made some paper pumpkins for our windows."

"Texas was the problem—instead you were licking Texas. Thanks for licking Texas."

Jude punched his pillow.

"What are you doing, Jude?"

"Nothing, just thinking ..." he said.

Often with all the lights out they would talk to each other like this before they slept.

"Someday all this will be a good story to tell *your* grand-children," he heard her say as prelude to a dream.

10

A Lucky Fish

An old weather proverb predicts changes after a full moon, and after Halloween, Hawkers Park had no rainy days, while Jude for the first time in his life was given a detention and made to stay after school, a punishment he felt quite pleased with himself for deserving. Of course, he missed his bus ride home after spending a half hour in the library under Mr. Port's watchful eye. Then when Mr. Port left for the day, he escorted Jude to the high school office where Principal Willoughby's secretary supervised the rest of it, the minute of Jude's release coming just as a Cobb Construction dump truck arrived to take him home.

On their way to the high school office, Mr. Port had concocted a mixture of gentle criticism, reassurance, and congeniality, offering this cocktail to Jude while gazing straight ahead and making a point of avoiding eye contact. He spoke in a needlessly hushed tone, for the school hallways were empty except for a custodian guiding an electric floor polisher from side to side or an electric floor polisher guiding a custodian. This, like a great many things occurring in Jude's life these days, was a matter of perspective.

As if imparting a secret, Mr. Port said, "You're lucky you didn't get suspended for all of next week, after throwing a punch like that. I would think your previous good behavior record saved you. And then of course there was the distraction simultaneously in Geometry class, which drew attention away from you and pointed an accusing finger at your victim. In fact, it looked like you were defending Mr. Evanson. Hmm, I'd say you were a lucky fish. A *lucky* fish," Mr. Port repeated, "Hmm."

He opened the office door and stood aside so Jude could swim in while he remained in the hallway. Set on a corner with two walls of windows exposed to hallways, the outer office did resemble a large aquarium with an ungainly philodendron crawling across a shelf top serving as an aquatic plant.

"Well, so long, Jude," said Mr. Port with the sort of sad smile that undertakers use when escorting the bereaved.

"A perch, I think," said Jude, "not just any fish."

"Of course," said Mr. Port, not knowing what to make of it.

Jude's punch had landed squarely on Peter Johnson's nose, with enough conviction to make it bleed and enough force to have broken it, except for Jude's newfound luck. This had come in the hallway outside Geometry class when Jude stepped behind Ronny Faber, grabbed his shirt collar and stuffed the wad of paper streamers from the Perch so far down his shirt back that Ronny had to reach under to pull it out from the bottom.

While he was engaged with this, Peter Johnson wheeled around to confront Jude, and took the punch Ronny might have gotten had he been less preoccupied with the sixty feet of streamer having *Sing, Baby Sing!* written its length every foot of the way as it came out of his shirt in a single stream coiling into a cone-shaped pile on the floor.

Needless to say, this mixture of paper ribbon, blood from Peter's nose, and various screams, whimpers, hoots, and shouts in the hall attracted Mr. Evanson's attention— as more luck would have it—a split second after he had noticed his classroom clock was missing.

Mr. Evanson found himself buffeted in a sort of whirlwind of school discipline breakdown with gales of misbehavior suddenly thrusting at him from all sides. Despite his steady geometer's habits, his head spun between the bare spot on his classroom wall where minutes before his clock had been hanging and the clock which mysteriously reappeared mere seconds later sliding out from under Peter's jacket when he let go of it to comfort his bleeding nose. Mr. Evanson didn't know which way to turn, so in fact he turned every which way.

If he had taken note of the pile of paper streamer on the floor, he might have come to a different conclusion, but the clock was all he could think of, most understandably because it was *his* clock and its theft a violation of *his* classroom domain. So it immediately struck Mr. Evanson that Jude had been defending the domain, taking the law too much into his own hands so to speak, embracing vigilante justice, but nonetheless succeeding in recovering his clock.

All this made its way into his report on the incident, which biased as it was in Jude's favor, and further supported by Peter Johnson's rapid recovery, led to both boys getting an hour's detention, no more. Since it also led to more or less the cancellation of geometry class that afternoon, happiness rather than gloom prevailed among Jude's classmates. Mandy Gordon even looked at Jude with something approaching amazement.

Later, Jude told this story twice, in two separate versions, neither one resembling Mr. Evanson's official version.

First to hear it was George Cobb who had been sent by Phyllis to give Jude a ride home when he missed her bus, and she subsequently learned of his being involved in an "incident" at school.

Jude's version for George as they roared along through Twin Rivers and then north toward Hawkers Park had to be shouted so George could hear it above engine din, a vibrating gear shift knob, rattling windows, and the occasional banging of the truck box when they flew over a bump. Jude had no idea dump trucks could go this fast.

What George heard was the bloody version with most of its thirst for vengeance, the triumph of good over stupidity and nastiness, leaving out only Jeannie T's indirect involvement in it.

George loved this version. He seemed almost to lick his lips from one detail to another, and sometimes asked Jude to repeat things, as if he hadn't quite heard them above the din, when in fact he loved them so much, he wanted to hear them again. "And you really socked him right smack in the schnozola?" asked George after he had heard that part of it twice.

Still later, at home for the evening, Jude's mother got the version that in movie rating terminology might be described as for *parents with children*.

There was much less blood in this version and not so much revenge as a desire to achieve understanding and get things behind him as far as Peter and Ronny were concerned. Mr. Evanson's clock loomed larger than it had in

George's version where it had seemed more a digression from the main point.

There was sufficient truth in Jude's tale as his mother heard it, that it didn't seem at all like a lie. It was even true that he and Peter Johnson had seemed to clear the air a bit while they sat together in Mr. Port's library, for a time sharing their detentions. At least it was true that Peter seemed cowed and subdued and sometimes glanced Jude's way as if fearing another assault. After all, it had been a pretty good punch.

What Jude's mother made of her version was much less clear than what George Cobb made of his. Jude was relieved to note that the faraway look had not come into her eyes. She didn't ask him to repeat things, and when he was finished she said simply, "Be careful, Jude. Don't let your feelings get the better of your judgment." That was all.

As for changes in the weather … the rain had stopped so suddenly, one might have thought some hand turned off a spigot and then flung a window open to let more cold in. The occasional drying winds of early autumn were succeeded by chill, gusty ones day after day, till leaves that had once been the soggy carpet on Jeannie T's hill had blown down into the ravine on the other side, every one of them. So long as one remained up there somewhere, it seemed, the wind kept on blowing, as if they were candles on a birthday cake.

On Jude's treks back and forth he might have seen them tangled into the brushy undergrowth of hazel, Juneberry, and dogbane along the ravine edge, clinging there like refugees on a gunwale. He didn't notice, so intent he was on the task, on getting it over and getting on with other things.

He lowered his head and leaned into the wind, cold enough now that he cupped his hands over his ears and pulled up his jacket collar to warm them. Out of sight and out of mind far below him in the ravine the North Crow River still gushed with springtime force.

Above him the Woodcock stood in a crosshatching of bare tree trunks and branches. He could see it from farther away than ever, with its lights on already as dusk creeping up the hillside almost beat him there. Since he could also see her car parked by the door, what was the point of going any further? He didn't have to walk the whole way, but he walked the whole way. He climbed her hill and came on till he was close enough to hear her singing. He couldn't explain why, and nobody asked him why—he just did it.

So the sky would darken with him eavesdropping on Jeannie T who often seemed to walk around while she practiced her songs. This he surmised since while he stood there motionless, the songs would sometimes be near, sometimes far away and hardly to be heard. Sometimes with her back to him, sometimes facing his way, she sang and Jude stayed, listening when long ago he could have gone home, when he was tired, shivering half frozen, and nearly late for supper. He stayed as if spellbound, or perhaps duty bound, trapped either by enchantment or obligation. It was all the same at this point, just as long as nobody asked him about it.

Finally came a string of warm days. Late autumn usually has a few summer afternoons up its sleeve, times when it's easier to ignore problems, so far away they suddenly seem, when you don't have to be crazy, or under a spell, or under somebody's thumb to hang around in some comfortable spot you've found.

The Twin Rivers *Daily Dispatch* in the high school faculty lounge pronounced it *Indian Summer*. Mr. Martin Evanson, ever alert geometer, noted this as a fact by tapping the very headline with his index finger, reaching over the shoulder of Constance Greshmer to make his point.

"I just love this time of year," said Miss Greshmer with a sigh. Then she noticed a paint smear near Mr. Evanson's fingernail.

"Could have gone duck hunting, but painted my porch railing instead," said Mr. Evanson.

"Set up my easel in the backyard, and painted a garden scene," said Miss Greshmer.

At day's end gunshots echoed from marshes beyond the ravine. Seconds later, a few ducks wheeled overhead. A wave of migrating blackbirds crisscrossing the marshes divided into two ribbons over hunters far below, and then came together to perch in trees over Jude's head. Their busy chirping all but drowned out a song about *songbirds no longer singing,* which the blackbirds seemed intent on disputing, as if in their raucous behavior was anything resembling birdsong at dusk.

Then there was supper—he would be late if he lingered longer. Still he lingered a little longer with his thoughts racing home ahead of the rest of him.

Why is it that so much seems possible if only things like supper and another day at school weren't waiting, and if people like Mandy Gordon, Peter Johnson, and the skinny man at Twisters would just mind their own business and leave you alone?

Another gunshot and a shout from out in the marshes took the place of an answer.

But something always comes between you and yourself. One day it's a grinning teacher's face, others it's a pork chop and a few peas, a retired professional wrestler, and hunters in the distance.

That last shotgun blast had made up the blackbirds' minds. Away they flew, and Jude headed home.

Earlier in the afternoon, Mr. Evanson had finished his latest visit to the faculty lounge by noting how restless his geometry kids had been with Indian Summer in the air, all except for Jude Henley, he noted. "I actually caught him nodding off in the middle of a theorem."

"I don't know him," said Miss Greshmer. "He's not in any of my classes, but I know *of* him. His mother is friends with the construction company Cobbs. My sister-in-law Debby drives buses same as Phyllis Cobb. Phyllis' friend Kate Henley and her son are living out in Hawkers Park these days."

"Not far from one of my favorite hunting spots."

"It's all owned by that retired wrestler Harmon Grove."

Mr. Evanson had never heard of him.

"Never heard of *'Alarmin Harmon'*?" This possibility amused Miss Greshmer.

Mr. Evanson began nibbling at the paint spot on his index finger. "It's all small-town stuff," he said. "One of these days I'm going to have to go somewhere where not everybody knows everybody. It's all too connected."

"I like it that way," said Miss Greshmer.

Mr. Evanson shifted to what was for him a safer subject—educational psychology, the 'pop' sort. "I guess I won't mind seeing the first snow," he said. "Kids knuckle down for a while once the ground turns white."

11

Hits and Misses

A week before Thanksgiving, Mr. Evanson got his wish. The season's first snow, three inches of it, fell while Jude got ready for school, and melted—most of it—by the time he stood in the cafeteria lunch line. Notwithstanding Mr. Evanson's educational psychology, nobody knuckled down.

Instead the first snow created pandemonium at Twin Rivers High. This spilled over into the cafeteria where, in the absence of snowballs, a mashed potato fight ensued, with dollops propelled from the ends of plastic spoons, all this quelled by the greatest eruption of administrative temper Jude had yet witnessed.

Principal Willoughby, hardly ever seen in the cafeteria, was only half seen now. Speaking from a safe haven behind the salad bar, he grew in turns incredibly red and then incredibly pale, seemed on the point of explosion and then on the point of collapse. He trembled from rage, from an agitated ulcer, and from having discovered his hand in a dressing bowl. Mr. Evanson waved his arms and seemed not to notice potato on his lapel. Mr. Port appealed for calm with a gentle reminder concerning the history of potatoes, how they actually had been first cultivated by American Indians. Principal Willoughby stared at him in amazement. Miss Greshmer thought she would have a gin-and-tonic when she got home.

Consideration was being given to cancellation of the Christmas dance. A hush descended. Sobriety ruled then for what remained of the day. Rumors were whispered outside lockers. Even Ronny Faber felt confidential, even around Jude.

"Do you think they mean it?" he asked.

Happy to be included for once, Jude said he thought they didn't. This would turn out to be a lucky guess.

Mere traces of morning snow remained in cool shadows later that day when he walked along the eastern base of Jeannie T's hill. Stooping, he scraped up enough to make a snowball, equal parts snow, sand, and rotting leaf, which he threw out into the ravine where it splattered against the arching trunk of a basswood precisely where he aimed. A red squirrel raced away among the treetops to another hiding place.

Lucky hit, thought Jude.

He wasn't always this good at lucky guesses and lucky hits. He couldn't have seen these as suggestions of things to come.

He stayed long enough behind the Woodcock to observe what might have been the last of many flights of geese he'd seen over Hawkers Park that autumn. Like most of the others, these followed the river eastward across the park, over the ravine, and then out across the marshes where the river meandered south. But this flock flew much higher than any of the others. These geese seemed not to share with their many predecessors any interest in what lay so far below them, the water and grassy cover which had been invitations to linger when nights were warmer and signs less clear to bird and boy that winter was at hand. Distant cries mixed with the singer's song and seemed to carry its words away with them, out of sight and finally beyond hearing in the darkening sky where occasionally a white wing flap caught a last ray of sunlight.

Threading his way back through the park with a flashlight growing dimmer by the minute, Jude passed the Rabbit, the Duck, the Crappie, and the other cabins, giving each no more than a glance. Doors and windows would be locked and closed, just as they had been the day before, the day before that, and for two months before that. The cabins were always the same and seemed no more likely to change than cubes in his geometry book, an exercise at the end of chapter six and his homework for the evening.

While spending the winter in the Bass, Harmon's drifter must have broken the table legs and sawed his bed in half because he couldn't think of anything else to do. He too was losing his mind. Already an intruder, he might have found himself hoping for the excitement of a further intruder, a broken window pane and a lock someone else had forced. He might even have wanted to study geometry.

Between the Woodcock at one end and their Perch at the other, everything was now black, with night not so much descending upon it as seeming to rise up from the earth and swallow it. Jude hurried along in a race with his failing flashlight batteries. Up ahead a slash of light from their kitchen window fell upon a wooden picnic table leaning on its side against a tree where Harmon had left it. There were twelve picnic table in all scattered throughout the park, all leaning against trees to protect their tops from winter weather. Jude had actually counted them and could have drawn a map pinpointing the location of each.

A shadow stirred across the slash of window light. It wasn't much of a shadow, but something moving nonetheless. With Harmon's drifter still in his thoughts, Jude snapped off his flashlight, less interested in seeing than in not being seen. If not the drifter returning, then maybe it was Peter and Ronny with another prank in mind. He wasn't confident punching the drifter would have quite the same effect it had on Peter Johnson, so he found himself favoring his annoying classmates as the explanation. A second later a skunk loped through the light, shambled past the picnic table, and disappeared into the night. Jude started breathing again, just as the first odors drifted his way growing stronger with his every step toward the Perch and near their door becoming a withering cloud.

Kate hadn't looked up from the kitchen table when Jude came in and brushed past her. "I have another letter from Harmon ..." she said, straightening up suddenly.

"— Jude, what is that awful smell? Is there a skunk outside?"

He didn't have to answer.

"You smell like you tried stuffing it in your pocket! It didn't bite you, did it?"

"This one just ran away."

Minutes later, when Jude looked up from his geometry book, mansion shadows danced in flickering candlelight. Tapers had been set out on the coffee table, the kitchen counter, and the table where his mother still sat.

"I read somewhere that burning candles will take away skunk odor," she said. "But so far it isn't working that I can tell—anyway it's pretty."

She had turned off all lights except for one over the range shining both on his cubes and supper cooking in three steaming pots. "Now our Miss Thorpe is two months behind with her rent. Any news from the Woodcock?" She glanced at Jude.

Jude shook his head. "You can see her lights from here."

"Harmon says she didn't answer the letter he wrote."

"She probably couldn't read his writing—the guy's illiterate."

"I doubt that's the case, Jude. I'm afraid what he says here is clear enough." She picked up the letter as if she intended to read from it, then changed her mind and put it down again.

Later they went outside, walked out into the park, and stood together looking at the lit windows of the Woodcock, two of them, one of greenish hue from a curtain pulled across it, the one Jude would sit under earlier in the season. The skunk odor had drifted away with the skunk.

"You really don't have to walk all the way up there if we can see so well from here now that the trees are bare."

"Harmon wants me to check the other cabins, remember? So I have to go almost that far anyway. And he wants me to get close enough to see what she's doing—in case she's moving stuff into her car."

"It's a ridiculous idea! If she did move out, what chance is there that you would catch her in the act? You'd practically have to live behind her cabin to have much of a chance of doing that."

Living behind Miss Thorpe's cabin wasn't far from the truth, as Jude saw it, so much of his free time had been spent there.

"And even if you did happen to be there the moment she picked for leaving, what are you supposed to do, grab her car keys and run, or throw your body across the hood of her car, so she can't see to drive? What Harmon really wants is to make us earn our rent following all his directions. He likes giving orders and making people hurry around." She had seldom been so hard on him, at least in front of her son.

"She was singing again tonight. She sings almost every night, the same songs over and over. You don't think it's *weird*, do you?"

"Of course not, Jude. People won't get anywhere with their abilities if they don't practice. A singer has to practice to keep a strong, healthy voice. Nothing weird about it."

Jude might have found this reassuring, except for being reminded of something—actually of two things: First, the words of the skinny man at Twisters when he tilted Wild Card after school on Halloween two weeks ago—*You can't win if you don't practice.* This in turn reminded him of *The Joys of Motherhood* still hidden away in Harmon's mailbox. One of these days he must remember to smuggle it back to the school library.

"I don't like this particular job anymore," said Kate. He could see both their breaths as they spoke.

She shivered and drew around herself the blue cardigan she had thrown over her shoulders. "I like it less every day, Jude. At first I didn't give it much thought. Harmon is so suspicious it's hard to take him seriously—sometimes I think wrestling affected his brain."

Jude thought he had been dropped on his head a few too many times.

Kate ignored this. "But all along he seems to have been right about Miss Thorpe, and that's what I don't like. It puts us squarely in the middle, between the two of them."

And it was just at that moment, with them in the middle, that everything turned black up at the Woodcock.

He thought of the geese flying south at nightfall, flying high and fast. Then Miss Thorpe's car started, chugging and clattering at first before quieting enough to be out of hearing from where they stood. Headlights flashed through the tree trunks and sent shadows leaping across the park as she turned around to go down her driveway.

"This doesn't mean anything," said Kate, whispering it so strangely that her son doubted she meant it. In fact, given the direction their conversation had just taken, she found the coincidence—for coincidence it was—unsettling. "She's going out for the evening, as normal as practicing her songs. Jude, you're getting as suspicious as our landlord—I'm sure the potatoes will be burnt."

All was now dark and quiet even on the far end of the park. They went inside where the potatoes weren't even close to burning and where Harmon's letter lay both in the center of their table and the center of their thoughts while they ate.

Jude finished the dishes and then Mr. Evanson's cubes just as the candle nearest him was burning itself out. His mother's room was dark. He slid between blankets spread out on the sagging couch and closed his eyes.

In a dream just begun, his mother's voice came to him at first as the words of a Twin Rivers High teacher. "He'll be locking her out when he gets back—if she doesn't run and beat him to it—and keeping her things till she pays up.

It isn't legal to do these days, but Harmon's a big property owner around here, and he has a lot of important cronies from his wrestling days. He'll try it I'm sure, and he might even get away with it. Do you hear me, Jude?"

"Yes," he managed to say.

"And *weird* isn't any kind of a word for Miss Thorpe. Maybe *unfortunate* is, maybe *sad* and *down on her luck*, but not *weird*."

Kate Henley had her own sense of justice to share with her son. Jude closed his eyes again.

Working by flickering light in an otherwise dark room must have reminded him of George Washington and Robinson Crusoe. He hadn't finished either, and they were due back. His geometry book had made a third in the pile on a corner of their kitchen table nearest a chair with his jacket hanging from its back. He remembered *The Joys of Motherhood* as the school bus door snapped shut behind him.

"Good morning!" chirped Phyllis. Peter and Ronny waved from the back. Jude's punch, another lucky hit, had the unexpected result of making them friendly—not friends, but still friendly.

12

Broken Stems

Thanksgiving vacation arrived without further snow. In the faculty lounge Mr. Port alluded to the tendency of things to begin one way and then end another. A winter beginning like this was certain to end with a flourish. Mr. Evanson viewed this as unscientific and superstitious. Flourishes had no place in geometry.

"I like them," said Miss Greshmer, "and also surprise endings." At that point and as if on cue Principal Willoughby walked in and asked where everyone was going for Thanksgiving. Since none of them were going any-where, this led nowhere, and Principal Willoughby re-turned to his office as much in the dark as ever.

The Henleys had been invited to the Cobb house for din-ner, and afterwards George—in a better mood than usual—took Jude for a ride across his fields on a yellow bulldozer. Eventually he let Jude drive it, working its levers to steer by slowing down one side or the other. Maneuvering this noisy, clanking hulk required a surprisingly delicate touch. Jude took them around in a series of circles resembling a penmanship exercise, each one with George in a laughing fit. With the bulldozer at last under better control and George merely grinning, they lowered its blade and scraped up a thin layer of moist, partially frozen clay, which folded over on itself like the ribbon candy Phyllis made for the holiday season, some of which Jude had been offered this very day.

At the end of a field, they clanked and rumbled straight out into a peat bog pushing over a dead willow in their path. Jude's instinct had been to dodge this, but as soon as he tried maneuvering out of its way, George's hand came down over his on one of the levers.

"No, let's go straight over the damn thing," he shouted above the whining diesel engine.

Jude, still without a sense of the power of this monster he drove, struggled with the impulse to duck and close his eyes as they hit the willow head on with a thud, then a crunch, then a crumbling sound as the whole thing went down in front of them, and they drove right over it.

George pulled a small bottle of whiskey from his back pocket.

"Take the levers again," he shouted, though by this time Jude already had both in hand again and was imagining what would happen if Harmon's cabin lay in their path. "Flat as a pancake," said George with the broken willow in mind.

"Flat as a pancake," said Jude with the Pike in mind and Harmon in it.

Behind them sprawled the broken willow, its bare trunk not resembling a pancake but instead a large bone, pulverized where the bulldozer tracks had run over it. George took a long swig of his whiskey and held the bottle between his knees while they circled out of the peat bog and clattered back across the field with a few crows wheeling overhead behind them as if the felled willow was a carcass they might feed upon.

George took another swig, a big enough one to empty the bottle this time. He threw it over his shoulder out on the clay field where it cart-wheeled and lay glinting in what remained of the afternoon's light. Straight ahead in the distance lay the low gray line of sheds where Cobb Construction kept its machinery. Beyond that, sprawling over a knoll of a few bare shade trees and mostly brown grass, the Cobb home awaited their return.

"Well, *Happy Thanksgiving!* I guess you might say, or words to that effect." George spoke with a drunken slur. He mentioned something about being forced to eat ribbon candy this time of year, and suddenly he wasn't so happy.

"Ribbon candy—I love that stuff," Jude said.

"What?"

"I was just thinking how much that clay we dug up looks like the ribbon candy Phyllis made."

"Tastes about as good too," said George. "I hate that shit."

"I like it."

"To each his own, I always say, or words to that effect."

"Come on, George, you know it's pretty good."

George scowled.

Jude always felt on inexplicably good terms with George Cobb, despite his glowering, changeable moods, his habit of rubbing his nose when he talked, and his whiskey. He thought he could say silly things to him—whatever came into his head—and George, who around his own house minded books so much, wouldn't mind at all.

George felt the same about Jude.

"Jeez," he said, how can you talk about food after that meal we just ate? I hate all that damn candy Phyllis makes. Almond bark, peanut brittle, penuche, marshmallow and coconut what-cha-ma-call-ums—I hate it all! She's always cooking it up and gorging herself on it. She's getting as big as a whale."

Soon they were all gorging themselves on the strawberry shortcake Phyllis set out for dessert when they returned from the field: three rich biscuits, three layers of strawberries, three of whipped cream, a tower. George's slur had become a singsong. His mood teetered back to jovial. And despite the sentiments he had expressed earlier, he attacked his shortcake with gusto.

"Where did you get strawberries this time of the year? I'll bet they're from Mexico, huh?" sang George.

"They're from the freezer," said Phyllis. "Before that, from your mother's patch last summer."

"I think they also grow them in California this time of the year," said George.

"I'm so glad we have tomorrow off," said Phyllis, turning to Jude, turning too obviously away from George who had just dropped a large berry on her white tablecloth.

"I wish somebody would give me a day off once in a while," he said. He had gone bulldozer fashion through his shortcake, leaving a string of strawberries across his shirt front like a willow toppled there.

"I wish I had a better job," Kate said, "As long as we're all wishing for something."

"Debby Connors was supposed to quit when she got pregnant," said Phyllis, "but now she's four months along and still driving. If she drove full term, there wouldn't be a month's work left for you at the end of the year."

"If she drives that long, she'll have her baby on the bus," said George, hitting a soprano note. "I think they also grow strawberries in Florida."

"I haven't got my license anyway," Kate said.

"Get it soon, will you?" said Phyllis. "You can never tell when Debby might quit. Her route is full of chuckholes."

"If she had her baby on the bus," said George, "they could name it Chuck, or better yet, *Bus*-ter."

Jude had never seen him more talkative. Kate wondered if she had ever heard him laugh before. Phyllis thought he had never been more embarrassing.

"It's easy to pass the bus driver's test," Phyllis said. "I should have given you help with it before this."

"What if the baby is a girl?" Jude asked George whose eyes ignited at that suggestion.

With his wife ignoring him more than ever, changing the subject all the time, he had turned to Jude. "They could even name a girl *Buster*—ever hear of a dancer by that name at a nightclub in Jeffers? The Purple Palace it is, and do you know why they call her Buster?" George winked.

"—George Cobb, don't you dare say!" Phyllis interrupted.

"I guess I can't tell you," he said, "at least not with ladies present." He made four falsetto syllables out of *ladies*, so that it sounded as if he were practicing a musical scale at the high end. He winked at Jude and began laughing with his hand over his mouth. He laughed till he shook. He laughed and shook till he choked and ran to the sink for a glass of water. Then with his back to them all, he laughed and shook and choked some more.

"What nonsense," Phyllis said.

"Ho! Ho!" gurgled George.

Phyllis stood up and swept away the dessert plates. From a china hutch which held her high school speech contest trophy, she brought out flowery cups and saucers and tiny crystal goblets.

With her back turned, George tried to get Jude's attention by holding his cupped hands at a considerable distance from his chest and making a motion suggesting a bra under explosive strain.

"Kate, I hope you don't mind if your son has a toast with us," she said. "It is Thanksgiving after all, and he is the man of the house."

"As long as we don't have to carry him home," she said.

"Ho! Ho!" gurgled George.

"Hold your liquor, Jude, do you hear?" said Phyllis, "and never drink so much that you make a spectacle of yourself." She glanced at her husband who returned to the table as she was pouring coffee into their cups followed by apricot liqueur into their goblets. "Are you better now?"

"Buster," he said. "That's about the funniest thing I ever heard, or words to that effect." He rubbed his nose, a very red nose with a white blotch on its bridge, and he raised his goblet with apricot liqueur shimmering in it.

"Happy Thanksgiving to our friends Kate and Jude," said Phyllis who at formal moments could seem so strangely formal for a woman who drove a school bus at other times and wore a baseball cap.

"To our friends Phyllis and George," returned Kate.

The amber liquid slid down Jude's throat like warm oil, leaving a sweet, pulsating trail behind it.

"Jeez!" shouted George. "Ah!"

He had lowered his empty goblet—not really all that hard, Jude thought afterwards—but its stem broke off regardless when it hit the table, and the rest of it rolled across to Jude just as the trail of apricot was coalescing into a burning globe in the pit of his stomach.

"Ah, Jeez!" from George again, as he jumped up with the goblet's severed base and stem still in hand.

"George, for heaven's sake get a grip on yourself," said Phyllis through her teeth. She jumped up after him and whisked away the part of the goblet that had rolled toward Jude. "Pretend you don't see any of this," she said to him and his mother.

Kate fumbling in her purse for a cigarette got a faraway look in her eyes.

"It's junk stuff," George said, handing her the rest of the goblet.

"It's my fine wedding crystal." She flung open her sink cupboard, revealing what might have been a small public library, and side-armed the goblet pieces into a plastic garbage bucket. She lingered at her china hutch while a wave of embarrassment passed over her, and then when she had recovered from that, she turned to her husband and whispered, "I'll get you another one."

"Don't bother," said George, after the fact, not whispering, sounding suddenly morose. "My hands were made for bulldozers, not for wedding crystal."

He held up his hands, palms out, and invited them all to inspect them, as if their fitness for bulldozers and unfitness for crystal would be immediately evident. But they weren't very large hands, and they trembled. It was hard to be sure what they were made for. Perhaps George was imitating something he had seen on television—where he got most of his ideas—something like the cowboy saying, "My hands were made for punching cows, Ma'am, not for holding babies." It seemed to George like a good thing for him to say at this moment, a thing that would explain what had happened, but it didn't work because his hands were so small.

Phyllis forced another goblet into George's small, trembling hand. "We have to have a respectable Thanksgiving toast," she said defiantly.

"What was wrong with the one we just had?" asked George who was still looking at his hands, as if they surprised him by not being very big and by not having as many calluses as he expected them to have.

"Our last toast," said Phyllis, pausing between each of her words, "wasn't quite respectable."

Kate lit a cigarette and stared at the floral design on her china cup. Jude stared at the red strawberry, a casualty lying on the battlefield that George's part of the tablecloth had become. George made a face at his wife and sat down.

"To our friends Kate and Jude," said Phyllis again.

"To our friends Phyllis and George," Kate replied, stammering this time.

Once again Jude's throat warmed. Another hot globe formed in his stomach. Then George's goblet broke, no mere accident this time, for he had snapped off its stem while drinking. The top of it fell to the floor and shattered. The rest he hurled against the dining room wall a foot over Phyllis' head. Jude noticed a trickle of blood around

George's thumb, a puff of plaster dust sifting from the wall behind Phyllis.

"George!" she shouted, but George was already out of the dining room, out of the kitchen, and slamming the back door behind him as Phyllis broke into tears. "Oh, he's so terrible, so unbelievably terrible!" she sobbed with her head down on the tablecloth.

Kate grabbed the bottle of apricot liqueur and poured herself another drink. She poured one for Phyllis and Jude. "Here, drink this," she said to Phyllis. "You'll be all right. Don't be upset—it's just one of those things that happens sometimes."

Kate drank. Jude drank. Phyllis came up for air and spilled hers down the bodice of her dress.

"I'm so sorry, Kate—Jude. I'm sorry. It's so awful," she sobbed. They both tried telling her that it wasn't awful, but *it was awful.*

Jude couldn't help liking George—and somehow still liked him—and so whatever they said to comfort Phyllis sounded phony. Twice his mother said, "We've had a wonderful time this afternoon, haven't we, Jude?" He tried agreeing, but his mind rebelled against the sound of it, hollow till he thought about driving George's bulldozer out there on that barren field and knocking down the willow, and then about their opinions of Phyllis' candy and everything else they had shared. Yes, it *had* been a good time, that part of it at any rate.

His throat burnt with yet another drink of apricot, this one poured so unsteadily by Phyllis that an orange wreath formed around his goblet on the tablecloth. He was having a terrible time all of a sudden. He felt dizzy with apricot, and he wished they could go home.

Gradually Phyllis quieted. She went off to her bedroom to change her dress.

Jude found it difficult to lower his goblet precisely within the orange wreath. Even with his right eye on it, he wasn't certain which way his hand would go.

When Phyllis returned in a fresh dress and face powder, she filled their goblets yet another time. Jude had lost count of all that he drank, but it seemed an apricot orchard.

"To my friends Kate and Jude," he heard her say again—from what seemed further away than the earlier toasts.

"To Phyllis," they both answered.

And to George, he thought, despite himself.

Outside in one of his sheds, George's bulldozer rumbled to life again.

"I'll take you home now," said Phyllis, still sounding as far away as the next room, but standing at Jude's elbow.

As they drove away in her gold Mercury four-door, Jude saw the rump of her husband's bulldozer back down among the willows at the edge of the bog. He seemed to be knocking the whole grove over. A few crows circled overhead in the deepening blue Thanksgiving sky.

Ten minutes later, he and his mother were alone back in the Perch, in their mansion. Jude lay down on the couch and slept away the rest of the afternoon, into an amber evening with a full moon slipping behind an overcast, his brain a tangle of thoughts about Phyllis, George, Miss Thorpe, Mr. Evanson at school, triangles and cubes, *The Joys of Motherhood*, and his stomach—a boiling pot of apricot stew.

He awoke once, with the couch rolling beneath him, having drifted out to sea with him upon it. The wonder was he became no sicker than this. His mother stood over him, unfolding a blanket from his toes to his neck, tucking the ends of it under the couch cushions.

"You weren't supposed to drink all that," she said. "You're such a man already, Jude, sometimes I forget how young you still are."

Then he started to say something about George Cobb, lost his way and fell back asleep in the middle of it.

So he didn't hear her say, "Good old Jude, always faithful." He didn't feel her hand brushing his hair back from his sweaty forehead.

13

Discoveries

Jude slept late into the next morning and awoke with Phyllis and his mother sitting at the kitchen table drinking coffee and talking in hushed tones that were still loud enough for him to hear as he lay on the couch.

"He's such a jerk," Phyllis said in what was more a hiss than a whisper. "George is a first class, dirty jerk."

"George just drank a bit too much yesterday. He doesn't do it often, does he?"

"No, but he's a jerk all the time." Phyllis' hiss became a whisper as Jude stirred beneath his jumbled blankets.

"How do you feel?" his mother asked him. "I let you sleep late—I thought you'd need it."

"I feel okay," Jude said because Phyllis was there, she being part of the reason he didn't feel okay. He felt crummy from yesterday's apricots.

"Hey, Jude, look what I brought to cheer you up," said Phyllis. Her words quivered with the false enthusiasm of someone eager to change the subject, in this case from drunken husbands and the liqueur she had irresponsibly poured down Jude. She bounded away to the curtains across from him, and when she drew them apart, a sunlit blaze of golden orange school bus filled virtually all of the latticed window panes. "I thought you might miss this old boat," she said, "so I drove it over here for you to look at on your day off."

Jude groaned and rolled to the inside of the couch. The couch groaned. "No, thanks," he said. "I see too much of that bus as it is." He rolled to the outside again and sat up. His aching brain seemed clogged with festering, rotted fruit pulp. The school bus, exactly the color of apricot liqueur, was enough to make him gag. He glanced longingly toward to the bathroom.

"Phyllis has to take her bus into Twin Rivers for a safety inspection," said his mother. "I'm going with her if you feel well enough to manage here by yourself." Kate still had that faraway look in her eyes.

"I'll be fine."

"You'll find sweet rolls on a plate in the bread drawer, oranges in the fridge, coffee warming on the stove—be sure to turn off the burner when you're done."

"I'm not exactly hungry," said Jude.

"How about the rest of yesterday's shortcake?" suggested Phyllis. "It's still good, and I brought it along this morning. I think your mother put it in the fridge—and don't forget the candy in the cupboard."

"Candy?" Jude felt himself turning colors, orange with the oranges, red with the strawberries, back to orange when he glanced at the school bus again, then the blue, green, and yellow colors of Phyllis' ribbon candy.

"Today begins the Christmas season, Jude. After Thanksgiving is candy time. I brought peanut brittle, walnut divinity, and pineapple-coconut bonbons—all you can eat." For Phyllis, hunger was a virtue and food its reward. This was true all the time. Add in the embarrassment and guilt from yesterday's fiasco, and Phyllis went right over the top—she had brought what seemed a truckload of candy.

"Thanks," Jude said, "but for some reason I'm not very hungry right now. Maybe I'll have some later on though."

"Oh," said Phyllis, disappointed. "Sure, you're probably still full from that big dinner you ate at my house yesterday. I'll bet that's it."

"You're right," said Jude, even though she couldn't have been more wrong. He ought to have been hungry, but the rotten apricots in his head had sunk into his stomach when he stood up, and now he felt like vomiting.

Phyllis put on her red baseball cap. Yesterday's dinner dress and formality she had exchanged for faded blue jeans, checkered shirt, and the nonchalant face she wore driving her school bus.

"I'm going to give your mother a driving lesson," she said. "I might even let her take a turn at the wheel." She took off her cap and pulled it down over Kate's head till its long bill hid her blue, distant eyes and most of her nose, and she resembled a tiny tropical bird with a grotesque red beak. "If she drives my bus, she'll have to wear this of course."

"If I wear this," said Kate, "I'll drive right into the first tree along the road—I can't see a thing, Phyllis."

Jude did his best to look amused, but he was temporarily beyond reach of Phyllis' humor, her horseplay, and her Christmas candy. He looked pained instead. His stomach hurt, and the cap, which gave Phyllis a jaunty look, merely revived earlier impressions of his mother's helpless side. It had the striking effect, both comic and pathetic, of large clothes on small people. "I hope you feel good enough for me to go," Kate fretted, still beneath the baseball cap.

"I'm fine. Don't worry about me."

"Jude, you can't tell a mother not to worry about her kids. Why, George's mother still worries about him, and if you ask me—" Here Phyllis stopped, on second thought sure that she didn't want to be asked.

They went outside and boarded the bus. Jude ran after them with a shopping bag of tool company advertisements.

"Didn't you want to mail these today?" He passed the bag through the double folding doors to his mother.

"In the excitement, I forgot all about them," she said. "It's New York and New Jersey, addressed last night."

What excitement? thought Jude.

Phyllis, settling behind the wheel, adjusted her baseball cap and snatched sunglasses hanging from her visor.

Jude laid around the Perch till he felt better. He didn't eat anything, but when he felt good enough to go out, he put an orange in his jacket pocket, and decided to try flying a kite George had given him yesterday at one of those moments when he teetered temporarily into a good mood. It seemed at the time like a not very flattering gift, suggesting to Jude that George thought of him as a little kid who still played with toys. This impression hadn't left him, but with the day off, nobody around, time on his hands, and nothing else in particular to do, he thought he might as well try it.

"Don't bother with kite string," George had suggested. "If you've got a fishing rod with lots of pretty strong line, use that. It's the best thing, and when you're done, you can just reel it in."

So Jude found an old fishing rod in Harmon's storage shed and set out for a meadow down the sandy road across from the Woodcock. It turned out to be the best of days for kite-flying, or just about anything else, one of those almost magically warm moments of very late autumn, when even the wind is warm—if there is one at all—and the ground is warm and dry, and the day seems enchanted because it comes at an impossible time when snowstorms are looked for instead. Every minute he was out there he felt better, stronger, more purged of apricot liqueur. It was a gift of a day, more replenishing than a mountain of Christmas candy.

High, wispy clouds crisscrossed the sky from east to west where they thickened into a filmy haze, while higher up between the feathery strands were deep blue patches like lakes amid snowfields, all this noticed by Jude because flying a kite turned his thoughts skyward even before he'd gotten it airborne. As he walked down the sandy road, the end of November sun shone with nearly summer brilliance from one of these blue lakes, turning everything to gold: the sand, the withered milkweed stalks either side, even the air itself. He seemed to walk through a golden halo. But from tangled shrubbery, as he neared Miss Thorpe's hill, chickadees sang their winter song.

In the meadow across from there, Jude unrolled his kite and stretched it over wooden struts. Printed across its pea-green paper was *Look Up Cobb Construction!* in large white letters. He tied it to his fishing line and ran off across the meadow with the pole high up over his shoulder. It soared and swooped erratically at the end of the nylon filament. With an east wind grown suddenly gusty, it was soon apparent his kite needed a tail. Jude was so busy keeping it up he didn't notice how Jeannie T had turned the tables and was watching him for a change, shielding her eyes from the sun. High up on the hill behind him she had paused beside her car.

He ran. He stopped to reel in line when the kite fell. He turned and ran again, stopped and reeled again. The shattered heads of pigeon grass whipped against his pant legs. *Look Up Cobb Construction* caught a lucky gust and rocketed skyward at last, a hundred feet of fishing line grew instantly taut, and Harmon's fishing pole bent and wobbled as if he had hooked a fighting pike somewhere up in that blue sky. Then, as so often happens in stories where the *Big One* got away, at the height of the battle, luck intervenes. Harmon's pole, brittle with age, broke in two. Line that might have been a violin string only a moment before grew limp as spaghetti. The kite plummeted, cart-wheeling into the crown of a burr oak on the edge of the meadow.

It was still there upside-down, like a flag of distress for Cobb Construction, when Jude ran off to see what had happened on the hill. At almost the moment his pole snapped, he had heard a thump, the screech of scraping metal, an engine racing, wheels spinning, and finally silence.

He scrambled over a barbed wire fence tacked to trees around the meadow, raced across the sandy road, and then along it on the other side a few yards to where the Woodcock's driveway entered. From the sandy road ran driveways to each of Harmon's cabins, each driveway longer than the last, and the last by far longest of them all because the road veered sharply away from the line of cabins as it approached the hill. Unlike the other driveways, which were flat or gently graded, the Woodcock's had been bull-dozed through the woods straight up the hillside to a front door.

One could see Harmon's heavy hand at work here, as well as his limited imagination, his oversized heart, and his wrestling technique. He wouldn't have wanted Jeannie T or anyone living there before her to waste their time in a lei-surely, scenic, curving descent through the hillside trees, meandering and contemplating the beauty of a larger tree that would be better knocked down than gone around. Yes, *better*. Better to figure out where the road was and to make a beeline from there to the Woodcock's door, knocking down everything in the way.

That was Harmon's style, and whatever hazards he left behind for those venturing on his efficient driveway, what-ever ugliness he left behind, time had only worsened. This had made him money as a wrestler. Here it saved him some, but the driveway was narrow and deeply rutted now, studded with washed-out boulders set at crazy angles by the bulldozer blade. Roots of trees growing alongside had been so exposed by erosion that some of them appeared to be growing in the air, like the tree roots of a sinister fair-ytale forest, enchanted and eager to snatch whatever dared wander near, which in this case was an old Buick.

Jude ducked behind a hazel clump where the singer's mailbox perched uncertainly atop a rusting steel post. He peered through branches to where she'd driven off her driveway halfway down on the right. Her car's bumper seemed to be hung up on an exposed tree root. An oily riv-ulet of gray smoke strayed downhill from its tailpipe. She studied her predicament with her hands on her hips and her back to him. Between Jude and this vision above him, a downy woodpecker tapped nonchalantly on the dead upper trunk of a jack pine. He hunched deeper into the hazel clump, hoping to escape detection if she stood up and turned around, but he nudged the mailbox with his shoulder, and its tin door swung open with the same rusty complaint he'd learned to expect from nearly everything Harmon Grove owned. The woodpecker ceased tapping, and of course Jeannie T looked back and saw him at once.

She called down to him. *Could he lend a hand?* These words, the first Jude had heard from her that weren't song, in his frozen state in the hazel bush, might have been stray pieces from some other puzzle box, not the one he'd been working on the past three months. He tried connecting them to the familiar songs he had heard from her. Nothing fit. Her voice seemed lower and huskier than when she sang. *Lend a hand?* In a flash, the past few three months rolled away, and Jeannie T became *Miss Thorpe*, a stranger once again.

It took him so long to shake off this feeling that she turned away with a shrug. In stages he became unfrozen, first his thoughts, which in a fluid state spilled off in all directions. He thought of running to her side. He thought of running away. He wanted to see her, and he wanted to hide. One second he was glad to be there, while the next he would rather have been anywhere else in this world. He could help her. In fact by this time—without her knowing it—he had the habit of wanting to help her and the feeling that this was what he was already doing. He could breathe again, but his heart was still frozen in his throat. He could move his arms, but his legs felt numb with Harmon Grove's dirty work. One second he wondered how he could meet Miss Thorpe with an honest face, and then it was Harmon Grove he couldn't look in the eye, Harmon asking questions he'd never be able to answer.

Somewhere in his future he knew there had to be such questions, and already they bullied and angered him. The woodpecker began tapping again. Miss Thorpe bent her shoulder to the left side of her car. The rivulet of oily exhaust slid like repudiation down the hill toward him. He couldn't bear it. He knew this was the way it had to be, even if his future would be full of lies. He would face Harmon when the time came. Today, this instant, *she* needed him— Miss Thorpe needed him— and he would help her, come what may. So he raced up the driveway to where she was trying to rock her car free from the tree root. Jude did the same, without at first saying a word to her, but they weren't in rhythm— when he pushed she let go.

"Wait a minute," she said breathlessly. "Let's get together on this, okay?"

Jude nodded, swallowed hard, and noticed with relief the absence of boxes piled inside her car, clothes hanging from hooks. She hadn't, at any rate, picked this morning to run away. At least he wasn't helping her do that.

In unison, they lowered their shoulders to the front of the car. Jude found a handhold under its bumper, set his foot against the exposed face of a boulder.

"Heave!" Miss Thorpe sang out. "Ho!"

After a fruitless half dozen of these, they let go and stepped back. The Buick, having lifted slightly, now settled down slightly without budging from its snag.

The looked at each other, caught their breath, then got back to their places and tried again.

"Heave! ... Ho!"

Jude dug the toes of his other foot into driveway clay and strained till his heart seemed likely to pop out between his shirt buttons. His face was hot—though no longer from embarrassment. With every *heave*, the car lifted back a bit, with every *ho* it settled down precisely where it had been to begin with.

"Heave! ... Ho!"

Jude closed his eyes, set his jaw, lifted and pushed again ... and again.

Miss Thorpe decided it was no use.

Jude let go and opened his eyes. She had climbed up on the driveway embankment, and now sat there above him with her feet resting on the hood of her car.

"I shouldn't have been in such a hurry," she said. "See what happens when you hurry." She spoke in gasps, as out of breath as Jude, stopping every two or three words, to suck in breath.

He climbed up beside her, but instead of sitting down, he stood there feeling awkward with his hands in his pockets, and his gaze on the top of her head and her coppery red hair, cut short enough to flair slightly into open curls at her jacket collar.

She was nothing like the woman he imagined all the times he had listened to her sing. On the one end of what he knew about women other than his mother, she wasn't a bit like Phyllis, and on the other end she was nothing like Mandy Gordon. Both Mandy and Phyllis could wear baseball caps, achieving remarkably different effects. Mandy looked cute and Phyllis looked funny—Miss Thorpe was neither of these. Mandy, the cheerleader might have sung out a *heave* and a *ho*, but you'd never catch her putting her shoulder to the front end of a car, and Phyllis—he was absolutely certain—by herself could have lifted Miss Thorpe's car from the tree root. So here was Miss Thorpe at last, not the Jeannie T he imagined drifting waif-like in song between the walls of her cabin, tougher than Mandy but not as strong as Phyllis, not cute and not funny but maybe pretty, more a mystery than ever, even out of her cabin and sitting just two feet away, a piece from a different puzzle box.

He was surprised at how much younger she seemed than his mother's stories required. She didn't look a lot older than the oldest girls at his school, but she was dressed older, in a fashion that struck him as stylish, with open-toed shoes and khaki slacks whose knees bore umber clay smudges now, and with a yellow satin scarf wound loosely around itself tucked under the lapels of her blue blazer. Gold bangles hung from ears and wrists.

From where he stood he could only see the perky indifference of her hair. He couldn't see the frustration in her face, her dark eyes flitting nervously from car to driveway to the sandy road beyond, to an appointment she was certain to miss beyond that, then to the toes of her shoes, then to the toes of *his* shoes planted nearby. She wiped her forehead with a handkerchief pulled from her jacket sleeve, and then she folded the handkerchief, pausing to examine in several places smudges of make-up there as if while looking at them she was giving herself time to consider something else.

"You're the one who's always hanging around behind my cabin, aren't you?" She asked this carelessly, while still examining her handkerchief and not looking up at Jude.

Somewhere overhead had the woodpecker been tapping still, and did it stop with Jude's stopping heart and then start up again when his heart faltered forward? "I think so," he managed to say.

And she said, having taken a moment to rehearse this part of it as well, "It's okay, really it is, so don't go running off when I need you. I like having an audience. If I minded you hanging around, we would have met long before this, on the first day I noticed you, a couple of months ago at least. The fact is, we almost met a week ago, the day it snowed. You looked so cold out there, I thought about inviting you in, but you were gone the next time I looked out." The frustration in her eyes gave way to amusement as she found something comical in this. "Wouldn't that have been funny, to invite you in when you looked so cold?"

He agreed without seeing her point.

"I mean, the landlord—what's his name?"

Jude gagged out the name of Harmon Grove.

"Okay, so Grove, this old wrestler guy, sends you down here to see what I'm up to, and then I invite you in to warm up. Don't you think that would have been funny?" She twisted her head to look up over her shoulder straight at him.

It would have been funny, but Jude needed time to see it that way, so instead of agreeing, he attempted a smile that felt like something he could peel off his face. He blushed and wondered why he wasn't running away. Then he be-

came aware of something truly odd, completely unexpected. *He wanted to stay.* Despite everything, despite the
embarrassment of having been caught sneaking around,
caught long ago without knowing it, despite his love of being unnoticed, he had actually liked it when she looked at
him. It wasn't in the least like the feeling of Mr. Martin Evanson's gaze settling upon him near the end of geometry
class. It wasn't like Mandy's Gordon's cold glance. Now
Miss Thorpe was looking back down the driveway again,
and he wanted her to look back at him instead. So it came
as a complete surprise to him when he found himself sitting
down beside her, with his feet next to hers on the car hood,
her shoes and his shoes alongside. He didn't want to run
away.

"Well, we don't have to talk about it now, or any time
even," she said, judging his discomfort by his silence and
his bright red ears and herself surprised when he simply sat
down. "Anyway … you're not exactly an enemy, are you?"

Jude got his wish. She turned to look him directly in the
eyes. "We're caretakers for half our rent," he blurted. He
thought it sounded foolish. It didn't explain anything.

Miss Thorpe already knew, having heard it previously
from Harmon Grove before he left last September. "He told
me that you and your mother, *the Henleys* he said, the Henleys would be looking after me. I didn't have to ask what he
meant by that because he didn't mention it as a kindness
on his part."

"I'm sorry," Jude said.

"Hey, don't worry about it." She put a hand on his arm.
"If it helps pay your rent, I don't mind. Like I said, I like
having an audience. I'm a singer, you know."

Jude nodded. "I like it too," he said.

"What?" She looked at him again.

"Being your audience, I guess." Here with Miss Thorpe was the same honesty he felt with George. He could say what he really thought.

She squeezed his arm, then let go. "The important thing right now is to get my car out of here. If my audience could find me a saw or a hatchet, we could cut that root. Can you find me one?"

He didn't know where, but he leaped back onto the driveway, ready to look.

"And if you get near a phone—I don't have one—call this number for me. I was supposed to be in Twin Rivers for an eleven o'clock audition. Ask for this man." She took a business card from her jacket pocket and handed it down to him. "Tell him I've had an accident, and I'll be late. Tell him I'll get there as soon as I can."

A hatchet? A saw? A telephone? Jude felt there was nothing he wouldn't do for her. He slid the card into his shirt pocket and ran down to the sandy road. As he was making the turn at her mailbox, she shouted after him. "What's your name—I forgot to ask?"

"Jude," he shouted.

She waved.

He sprinted back up the sandy road, past all the other cabins. The east wind was stronger now, not only gusty but suddenly cold. Gone was the golden halo of a nearly summer sun that had greeted him when he first set out this morning. Jude didn't notice the change in the air, the new chill it brought. His thoughts were elsewhere as he ran along. *Not exactly an enemy* wasn't how he wanted Miss

Thorpe to think of him. And he was *more* than her audience. He'd gone through hell at school on account of her, and he would go through more hell with Harmon Grove if it came to that. He had hated spying on her. He'd become her friend without her knowing it. He wanted to help (that much she should be able to see now). He had his sense of justice. Somehow she had to know the truth of all this about him, and he was reeling from two discoveries: first that what had been hidden from her through all these long autumn months was not the wrong he had done, but the things that already made him her friend. Then there was the feeling of her hand on his arm. She wasn't simply someone in his imagination. That was the other discovery he took with him as he ran along.

14

Storm in the Way

Thumping against Jude in his jacket pocket like a second heart beating was the orange he had taken with him this morning and not found a chance to eat. He ran till he was out of breath and sweating despite the sudden chill. He unzipped his jacket and walked till he was shivering and had enough breath to run once more. Then he ran again, with little flocks of chickadees and sparrows flying up out of the roadside brush and fluttering away into treetops as he sped among them. He ran past all the cabins, the length of the sandy road beneath a deepening gray sky, all the way out to the highway because there was neither hatchet, saw, nor phone in the Perch, and even if the first two might be in Harmon's storage shed, he needed a phone, so without stopping there he sped on.

He went to the phone booth outside Twisters Café whose gravel parking lot at noon held a dozen cars and pickup trucks. He dialed the number on the card Miss Thorpe had given him, the Purple Palace, a name he'd heard for the first time only yesterday when George Cobb chortled over the sleazy night club where the dancer Buster worked.

"Jiffy Cleaners, Barbie speaking," a shrill voice answered.

"Is this the Purple Palace?" he asked anyway.

"The Purple Palace?" A giggle. "Don't I wish, though! No, it's just good ol' Jiffy Dry Cleaners."

"This isn't 847-9200?"

"It sure isn't," said Barbie from a phone near the steam press, and there went Jude's only coins.

In Twisters Café where he sought change for a dollar, you could have gotten a free meal by just standing around and breathing for a few minutes. The noonday crowd filled every seat and frying hamburger and onions filled the air. Jude stepped up to the cash register at one end of the lunch counter. On the other end, on his tiptoes was the skinny man adjusting a television shelved among cereal boxes and cans of fruit juice. The twelve o'clock news was on, folding first left and then right diagonally across the screen. When the skinny man touched a knob, it straightened out. When he let go, the news folded over again, rolling up on itself like a delivery boy's newspaper.

"Just stand there and hold it—ha! ha!" shouted the man on a stool nearest Jude. It was Carl Connors, laughing through his nostrils now, chewing, holding a cheeseburger in one hand and a coke can in the other, shaking both with his laughter, Carl, husband of Debby who drove her school bus through chuckholes pregnant.

The skinny man put a can of tomato juice atop the television. He let go, and the picture straightened out. "Tomato juice," he said to the nearest customer on that end. "Tomato juice will always do the trick, not orange or grapefruit, just tomato. Figure that out if you can."

The customer shook his head, held out his coffee cup. The skinny man walked Jude's way along the lunch counter pouring coffee from a steaming glass pot. Carl peered through dark sunglasses which he more or less never took off, no matter how dark it was. He glanced first at the café door, then at Jude.

"Are you sure the door shut behind you?" he asked with a voice surprisingly smaller than he was, and when he saw for himself that the door was closed, he said, "It sure is a cold wind out there. Two hours ago it was a warm wind. The temperature dropped fifteen degrees since then. Did you know that?"

Thanks to the Cobb Construction kite, Jude knew about the wind, though whether warm or cold he'd been too busy to notice.

"Well it has. I've got a thermometer on my pickup driver's side window, and I know it was fifteen degrees warmer only an hour ago, for a fact. A blizzard is moving in, they say."

Carl's sunglasses were periods at the ends of sentences in the very large paragraph his face made. When he said *blizzard*, his glasses seemed to shrink and his face expand. It was a bloated paragraph of a face, slack-jawed, a face having much to do with chili of the sort in a bowl before him, with burgers in hand, with pies of the sort in a glass case across the lunch counter from him, and with a lot of lying around on couches watching TV after the compound-complex dinners Debby fixed for him.

Carl loved blizzards even more than burgers and cream pies. He relished the sense of urgency they created, the distress they could create, the opportunities for search and rescue possibly involving his 4x4 pickup parked outside. He especially loved the sense of purpose blizzards gave his life. Nor did it hurt that he could make money from blizzards, for pulling people out of ditches and other predicaments, for plowing out driveways and parking lots with the blade he could mount on the front end of his truck.

"Tomato juice always fixes that television," repeated the skinny man arriving on Carl's end of the lunch counter. "It straightens out the picture every time. Orange juice and canned beans won't do a thing for it. Figure that out if you can." He paused in front of the cash register and set the coffeepot alongside on the counter.

"Tomato juice—I hate the stuff," said Carl, finishing his coke." He picked up the coffeepot and poured himself a cup.

"Just help yourself," said the skinny man after Carl had already helped himself. "What do *you* want?" he asked Jude.

"I need change for this." He held out his dollar bill.

"For the jukebox, the pinball, or the cigarette machine? If it's for the jukebox, hold off till we hear the weather on TV—they say a blizzard's headed our way." Carl sat up straighter on his lunch counter stool, squared his shoulders, and swallowed the last of his burger in a very large gulp. "If it's for the cigarette machine, they'd better be for your mother. You're supposed to be eighteen to buy cigarettes in this state."

"It's for the phone outside." Jude laid his dollar on top of the cash register, but the skinny man ignored it.

"You're out of luck," he said. "If we're snowed-in here, I might run out of change before I next get to the bank in Twin Rivers. I can take coins out of the machines in here, not from the phone out there." He picked up the coffeepot and dangled it over Carl's cup. "Have enough, Carl?"

Carl grunted, taking a sip. "I could use a few more crackers though."

"But I've got to have change—it's an emergency."

The skinny man bent behind the lunch counter for Carl's saltines in cellophane packs.

"It's for the pinball, then," he said feeling desperate.

The skinny man with crackers in hand had moved farther away to the fry grill. He glanced at Jude over his shoulder between turning hamburgers with a spatula and scraping grease to one side. He came back with Carl's crackers.

"Hmm, doesn't add up, does it, Carl? First it's for the telephone, now all of a sudden it's pinball."

"I'll put *most* of it in the pinball."

"You're a liar, boy. You wouldn't stand here lying like that if your father was alive." He spoke as if no more could ever be said on that subject.

Jude's dollar slid off the cash register and fluttered to the floor. When he stood up from retrieving it, his face felt hot, and the skinny man was back at the fry grill dealing out bun tops from a package, tossing each one like a playing card over a sizzling hamburger patty. Carl munched his crackers and twirled a spoon in his chili.

"Which is it," he asked with a wad of cracker bulging in his cheek, "an emergency or pinball?"

"Miss Thorpe in the Woodcock has run off her driveway down on the far end of the park."

"Does she have a CB radio? We could call her from my truck— I've got forty channels."

"I don't think so. She drives an old jalopy."

"A few years ago, people used to put 'em even in old cars, CB was so big for a while. Everybody wanted one. People don't know what they're missing out on these days. Is she hurt by any chance?" asked Carl hopefully. Ever since last Christmas when he installed his forty-channel radio, Carl had been daydreaming about using it in a true emergency, saving lives with it, and making himself useful and heroic.

"No, she's all right," Jude said, "but her car is hung up on a root." Carl reached in his pants pocket and pulled out two quarters. He reached in again and pulled out a third, then a dime and some pennies, one of which rolled around his coffee cup before he slapped it down on the counter. "Close enough?" "Close enough," said Jude.

Carl tugged the dollar from Jude's fingers. "Too bad this gal doesn't have a radio. If she had a radio, she could have called me on mine. I could have helped her out in a jiffy. Radio is great for emergencies. People don't know what they're missing. Are you sure she isn't hurt, bleeding a little maybe? I could call the sheriff or the state patrol."

"She's fine." Jude slid Carl's eighty-eight cents off the counter. Carl munched another cracker, spooned his chili. Slowly, very slowly, the idea dawned on him that since he was here, not in his pickup, he wouldn't have heard Miss Thorpe's distress call even if she had a radio, and then since he knew about her trouble now, having heard it from Jude, she wouldn't need to call him on a radio regardless, and he could help her anyway. But he believed so strongly in an emergency *with radio* that it took him this long to grasp an emergency without radio.

He had almost arrived at that point when the skinny man next approached with the coffeepot.

"Got to run," said Carl waggling a hand over his cup. "Who was that kid?"

"Who?"

"The one who was looking for change."

The skinny man paused near the cash register, put down his coffeepot, and began to say something when he was interrupted by the television. Along the lunch counter, everybody stopped talking and every head turned to watch the weather.

"Got to run before this thing hits," said Carl as the forecast ended. He handed the skinny man a ten from Debbie's most recent paycheck, "Be back for my change in a few minutes."

Back outside in the phone booth, Jude dropped the first of his quarters among cigarette butts on the floor. He got the second one in, then the dime, and dialed the right number this time.

"Palace," a man answered.

"Is Mr. Dwyer there?" Jude read the name printed on the embossed business card. *Dusty Dwyer*.

"Who wants him?"

"I'm calling for Jeanne Thorpe."

The man left the phone with Jude listening to the sounds of the Purple Palace at midday. Here also was the buzz of talk about a blizzard. As if people were bees and storm a flower blooming, everywhere there was talk about the blizzard, and here glassware clinking, laughter, music, the churning and clunking of an automatic icemaker near the phone.

"You can't even see out the window, it's snowing so hard," somebody said.

"You're so drunk you can't see anyway."

Glancing from the phone booth, Jude saw a few snow-flakes in the air, but farther off in the direction of Twin Rivers a white sheet drifted his way.

"Yeah, Dusty here," said Dusty Dwyer.

Jude spoke quickly to the metallic-voiced Dwyer.

"So what am I supposed to do about it?" This was Dusty Dwyer's all-occasion response to things he wasn't much concerned about.

And since Jude wouldn't have dared tell Dusty what he should do, he merely added that Miss Thorpe would be there as soon as possible.

"Tell her to forget it. I've got better things to do than wait for some dame in a snowstorm."

"It's *Jeannie T*," Jude blurted, thinking perhaps he should have used her stage name to begin with.

"You call her what you want. I'll call her what I want." Dusty hung up.

Jude stepped out of the booth and hunched down to fish his quarter from the floor trash. He felt that he had just crashed head-on into an element of life that was utterly new to him and for which he was even less prepared than other things he had encountered recently. Dusty Dwyer wasn't a small-minded, selfish man like Harmon Grove, nor a moody man like George Cobb, nor a slow -witted man like Carl Connors, nor a man of petty cruelties like the skinny proprietor of Twisters Café. Dusty Dwyer was his first gen-uinely cold-hearted, ruthless man, a tough and cruel sort who was smart enough to know how far toughness and cruelty could get him in this world and had taken plenty advantage of that fact.

Carl, in his 4x4 pickup with twin antennae swaying from its cab sides, had spun all his tires roaring out of the café parking lot and down the sandy road toward the park. Snowflakes and ice crystal pellets suddenly filled the air, tiny flakes sticking to Jude's jacket and pellets striking him all over, stinging his face and bouncing away. By the time he set foot on the sandy road, Carl was already out of sight. Carl was car-lifting size. He probably had a chainsaw handy in case he needed one for an emergency. If he couldn't lift Miss Thorpe's car off the root, he'd saw it off. He might even chew it off before Jude found a hatchet and walked all the way back with Dusty Dwyer's message.

So Jude forgot about the hatchet and ran back with the message alone, hoping he'd get there in time, hoping that he wouldn't be robbed of a small further part in Miss Thorpe's rescue, but before he was even as far as the Rabbit and Crappie, Carl came booming down the Woodcock's driveway and turned up the road toward him with sand and ice pellets flying out from under all his four wheels. Miss Thorpe followed him down the hill but turned the other direction, where the sandy road swung out across the river on a wooden bridge, skirted the broad marshland, and curved southeast to Twin Rivers, a gravel shortcut most people avoided.

Carl sped by Jude on his way back to Twisters. He flashed his emergency blinker lights and grinned. He had a doggy sense of excitement. His radio antennae wagged like tails behind him. Except for his truck's tracks, the sandy road was already light gray with the snow and ice which crackled under Jude's feet as he struck out across the whitening meadow to retrieve the fishing rod and whatever was left of his kite. *Cobb Construction* flapped in pea-green shreds out of reach among oak tree branches, in ribbons from the barbed wire fence, and in tatters from withered milkweed stalks and hazel shrubs. Only its wooden struts and a few tenacious shreds dangled yet from the end of Jude's fishing line, so well had the wind done its work. Jude reeled in what he could, gathered the two pieces of Harmon's broken rod, and went home.

Out on the sandy road, Carl's tracks were soon blotted out. The Woodcock had disappeared. He could see a hundred feet ahead, no more. Looking through that hundred feet where familiar shapes were becoming unfamiliar, where already nothing looked as it had when he last turned his back on it, he wondered if he would ever have a chance to tell Miss Thorpe that he'd been her *friend* all along and not a spy. He couldn't see that far ahead either.

15

A Fourth for Cards

Storms coming after warm days are always as harsh as broken promises.

Somehow Phyllis and Kate made it back from Twin Rivers with snow falling three inches an hour in a northeastern gale and visibility so nearly zero that, as Phyllis said, "I don't think a bat would have known where to go." But her school bus at last got stuck making the turn from the sandy road, no longer sandy, to the Perch's driveway, no longer a driveway either. Though the bus was still there, no more than fifty feet away, Jude couldn't see it from his mother's bedroom window, and Kate said she couldn't see the cabin when they climbed out of the bus and broke their way, groping, through three-foot drifts to its door. Even now, an hour later, their pant legs were dark with wet beneath the knees, Kate's cheeks—normally so pale—were red as sunburn, and Phyllis' blue and white tennis shoes were hours from being completely dry on a newspaper laid out by the door.

Jude had lit the fire in their heater and was sitting in front of it, cross-legged on the floor, staring into the dancing flames as gusts tugged at them from the chimney and moaned through a blue stovepipe whose draft clanked between open and shut. Mostly he was thinking about what had happened between Miss Thorpe and him, but mixed up in these thoughts were the storm, Carl Connors, Dusty Dwyer, and now Phyllis. What would it be like to have Phyllis marooned here with them, for days perhaps?

Phyllis had already declared that she could drive no farther, wouldn't even try, was happy to be stuck right where she was, and didn't even think of it as being stuck. She tramped back and forth behind Jude in her stocking feet, and she spoke excitedly to Kate who sat in the sagging chair with one leg folded under her. About every five minutes, Phyllis peered out whatever window she happened to be near.

"Boy! You can't see a thing out there," she said almost every time she looked out and saw nothing but more snow. "We'll have to make the best of it," she said a couple times, as if that wasn't very bad at all. In fact, she was looking forward to making the best of it.

The stove draft clanked. Ice pellets were flung like sand against their rattling windows.

"Won't George worry?" asked Kate.

"Kate, since yesterday, George can jump in the river for all I care. He might have scalped me with my own wedding crystal." A window curtain muffled her voice. She drew away and flung herself full length on Harmon Grove's couch. She gazed up at the ceiling with her hands behind her head. "This couch doesn't stop sagging till it hits the floor," she said. "Can't old what's-his-name find you a better one?"

"He promised," said Kate, "but that's as far as it went."

"I wouldn't think it a hard promise to keep unless it's the same old stuff in all the cabins. They're all vacant now, aren't they?"

Kate told her about Miss Thorpe.

"Jeanne Thorpe," said Phyllis wistfully. "God, she has a pretty voice. I haven't heard her since a year ago last summer. She sings a lot in some of the resort nightspots where people our age hang out, where George and I go when he's not breaking my fine wedding crystal. What's she doing up there?"

"I think she's a little down on her luck at the moment," said Kate. "All those summer places are closed up this time of the year, and I suppose singing jobs are hard to find. She's two months behind on her rent, going on three."

"I'm really sorry to hear that," said Phyllis. "She has such a lovely voice, though it's the sort that us old fogies would like, not teenagers like you, Jude." She glanced Jude's way.

Jude had his back to her and his face to the fire. From elsewhere than the fire he felt a wave of warmth.

Phyllis, with difficulty, sat up on the sagging couch. With much less effort, she rested her chin on her knees. "I wonder if she'd like to come down here for cards. Jude is three, and she could be a fourth for Five Hundred or maybe Euchre."

"It's over a half mile to her cabin," Kate said. "I doubt that she could come so far in this storm, even if we had some way of getting in touch with her, which we don't. I've wanted to invite her here before this, but it's awkward to do it now, with her rent problems and us supposed to be caretakers."

"Yeah," said Phyllis, "you wouldn't want her to think that you were prying or trying to pressure her I guess."

"She isn't home anyway," said Jude without turning around. "She drove into Twin Rivers just after the storm began."

"Lord! Jude, I hope she made it," said his mother.

"I just love Euchre," said Phyllis, flinging herself back down on the couch, "but it isn't much fun with three—you have to have a fourth."

Jude thought he heard something other than the wind outside, something between thunder and an earthquake. Phyllis leaped from the couch and ran to the nearest window. She swore and buried her face in curtain pleats as the sound deepened into a pulsating throb, more mechanical than natural, and became finally the roar of a very large engine.

"Why did he have to do it?" she sobbed. "Why couldn't he just leave me alone for once? We would have gotten along just fine marooned here, the three of us."

Outside the Perch's main room window, an enormous pea-green form heaved into view through sheets of blown snow. It flashed blue and yellow lights, and its tires were nearly as high as the cabin eaves. It was an earth loader, an elephant of a machine, designed for labors in swamp muck or polar ice. Its diesel engine idled down to a slow, rafter-shaking rumble, Kate opened the door, and with a gust spraying snowflakes and ice crystals through the room, George Cobb of Cobb Construction stepped in, a fourth for Euchre.

"I've come for Phyllis," he announced almost formally, without a greeting first and speaking from the puffy cave of a blue, goose-down parka with its hood drawn up in a tight circle that hid the lower half of his face. His face couldn't be seen at all, except from straight on, and then it seemed a preposterously small face for one who piloted the green elephant outside. Nor could Phyllis be seen—from any angle— for she had withdrawn into the bathroom and closed the door.

"They told me at Twisters that her bus turned in here over an hour ago…. How she made it this far, I'll never know. Nothing's moving out there." He went on like this, as if Jude and his mother were hiding Phyllis, and he had to explain how he was wise to their game. When he nudged her tennis shoes drying nearby, a cake of compacted snow slid off his boot and fell into one of them.

"I'm as good a driver as you any day," said Phyllis from the bathroom. "That's how I made it this far, George Cobb." Her sorrow of the minute before had turned into rage.

"Maybe then you could have made it the rest of the way home," George shouted at the bathroom door. "Maybe you don't like it around your own house."

"Maybe I don't!" shouted Phyllis.

"Won't you sit down, George? Don't worry about getting snow on our floor." Kate invited him toward a kitchen chair, but George was as far from worrying about snow on the floor as he was from sitting down. "Phyllis had to bring me home. Jude would have been left alone here otherwise, for days maybe, and without a phone," she explained. "I went into Twin Rivers with her this morning."

"I figured as much," said George, still not sitting down, "but there's friends and there's family …." He held out his two mittened hands. When he noticed his mittens, he pulled each off with his teeth. This exposed the small, trembling hands he had held out only yesterday over the

Thanksgiving table, and with the fingers of one standing for friends, he tapped the palm of the one standing for family. "And where I come from, family always comes first."

"Of course it does, George, of course," said Kate with soothing tones.

"Shut your mouth, George. Shut your stupid mouth!" shouted Phyllis, still behind the door.

"Twenty people are marooned up at Twisters," continued George, "a dozen at the café and two families across the highway in the church. Carl Connors is stuck crossways in the ditch with most of his pickup buried. Carl begged me to pull his truck out and into the parking lot. I have the only machine that can move in a storm like this, but I turned them all down. I came here for Phyllis instead, because family always comes first as far as I'm concerned."

The bathroom door opened slowly. Phyllis walked out with frozen composure no weather could have achieved. She put on her baseball cap which hung from a hook behind the cabin door. She put her foot without flinching into the tennis shoe where George's snow had fallen. Water seeped through its seams and squirted over its sides.

"Don't you have a coat?" George asked, suddenly sounding timid.

"I have my heavy wool shirt," she said. "It was fifty-five degrees when I left home this morning. The sun was shining."

The Cobbs had been dramatically quieted by the sight of each other. They were speaking in hushed tones now, like people at the scene of a car wreck.

"Here, wear this," said Kate. She draped over Phyllis' shoulders an old muskrat coat that had once belonged to

Jude's grandmother and now sometimes served him as an extra blanket.

"Thanks, Kate, thanks for everything," said Phyllis, beaming gratitude. "Thanks, Jude."

George muttered something muffled and thankful sounding from back within the cave of his parka hood. He and his very large muskrat pushed outside into waist-deep snow.

"We'll come back for the bus as soon as this wind dies down," shouted George over his shoulder. A gust caught his words, blowing most of them away before they could be heard. Kate heard *wind*. Jude heard *bus*. Neither heard *dies*. A minute or so later, the pea- green elephant rumbled away from their windows. They glanced at each other before Jude turned back to the stove.

"He almost brained her at dinner yesterday," said Kate, more to herself than to Jude, for normally—in front of him—she avoided taking sides between Phyllis and George. But she was agitated. She had that faraway look in her eyes. Without turning around, Jude knew it had to be there again. "He almost brained her yesterday, so that's how much family comes first with him. —Jude, why do you just keep sitting there, staring into those flames?"

He spun to face her without getting up. "Fire is so interesting," he said.

"So is my son," she said. "Tell me how you found out Miss Thorpe went to Twin Rivers."

16

Jude, Not Judas

For the next three days snow piled up outside and wind from various directions piled drifts around the Perch and the other cabins and then rearranged them. Time for Jude seemed to pile up inside as well and to stack itself around him in various arrangements. He soon discovered he had much more of it than he needed; for spending with his school books; for listening to the wind and watching flames dancing in the round, smoky window of the cabin heater; for helping his mother get so far ahead with her tool company mailings she would have nothing to do next month. Neither of them could talk from licking so many envelopes. They were snowed in, and Miss Thorpe was snowed out. As the storm abated, visibility improved, and another night descended, it was possible to see that windows remained dark on her hill.

She was marooned in Twin Rivers. Of course she had missed her audition, but she hadn't left the Purple Palace empty-handed, for she was more capable and self-reliant than Jude could have imagined. She won from the ruthless Dusty Dwyer another chance at least, in a month when he would next need a singing act for his club.

So Jude's Thanksgiving vacation and Jeannie T's trip into Twin Rivers lengthened in tandem, into Monday when the Twin Rivers schools were closed on account of the blizzard, and into Tuesday when they were open but buses weren't running out into the country yet. Late Monday afternoon, a county snowplow cleared the sandy road, breaking through drifts of eight feet, and sometimes backing up to have second and third runs at them. In its path on both sides, it buried what wasn't already buried of tree trunks and brush and mailboxes at the ends of cabin driveways. The sandy road was almost a tunnel now, and through this tunnel with night settling in came an old Buick, left parked at the foot of the Woodcock's unplowed driveway. Minutes later lights were on in the Woodcock again.

Outside at that point, Jude took note and felt a wave of relief. The sky clearing toward dusk had become as absolutely blue as only a snowstorm can leave it. He had gone out to see what the plow had done. Just getting outside had turned out to be challenging, with their doorway blocked and shovels a hundred feet away in Harmon's shed beyond a door even more blocked. Getting there at times seemed more like swimming than walking. But in places wind had packed the drifts so hard he could stand upon them and bring his eyes even with the cabin eaves and the large lower branches of trees. It was a strange feeling, as if suddenly he had grown three or four feet, or the world had sunk by that much. Time after time a crystal surface crunched and crackled beneath his boots, then fractured and collapsed beneath him. Snow shot up into his pant legs and coat sleeves. His eyes found their usual level. He would push off once more with his arms flailing, his chest pushing into the snow, then find a firmer patch and rise, then crash through again. Several more such episodes brought him at last to the door of Harmon's storage shed.

On the trek back, following the trail he'd broken and with a snow shovel in hand to prop him up, he paused once more to note the lights of Miss Thorpe's cabin. From out in the ravine an owl hooted, waited, and hooted twice more. From another sector came another set of hoots. A pair of owls, it seemed, exchanged reassurances as darkness settled. Jude himself felt reassured. The air was perfectly still now. A column of smoke from their cabin chimney formed a straight line to a thousand stars.

"I'll dig out the mailbox tomorrow morning," Jude said when he was inside again and warming himself near the heater. "Miss Thorpe is back."

He felt flushed and breathless pulling off his boots and shaking snow from his socks. He'd been outside only a few minutes, but long enough to take his breath away, half of it from his exertions, the other half from simply the excitement he discovered there.

That's the way it is with a blizzard and even more so, its aftermath, a world suddenly transformed and becalmed beneath a snow blanket, a world offering illusions of change and new perspectives. Angles had been softened, rooflines obliterated, and picnic tables buried. From out of nowhere the broad sweeping curve of a snowdrift unfurled between suddenly shortened tree trunks where before there had been simply a flat expanse of park land and taller trees. Old paths were hidden and new ones forming, his own to the storage shed, then out to the sandy road. A rabbit had crossed their yard on that side. New journeys could

be made through a new world with every step of every creature a record kept, its own diary. He would look out next
morning and see still where both he and the rabbit had
journeyed today. Snow lumps from his socks turned instantly to steam on the heater grill—even that was exciting.
And Miss Thorpe had returned.

Next morning as he made a new path through drifts out
to their mailbox, George Cobb and an employee named
Clarence arrived in the earth-loader to free Phyllis' bus.

"Well, it's back to school for you tomorrow," chortled
George with his usual dim view of other people's vacations.
He kicked snow from under the bus bumper, and bent low
to fasten a log chain.

Clarence fastened the other end, winding the chain several times around an arm of the loader's bucket, then hook-
ing it through one of its own links. "We knew you'd be
happy to see us," he said, "so we beat it right over here." He
laughed and spit tobacco juice, a brown stream, through
the gap of a missing tooth.

"You don't have to rush on my account," said Jude.
"School can wait a few more days. As far as I'm concerned,
it can wait till after Christmas."

"And all the while I'd have my old lady around the house
bugging me instead of driving this," said George. "Thanks,
but no thanks! Let's get this baby on the road again, Clarence, so Jude can get his education, and I can get a little
peace of mind."

Clarence laughed and winked at Jude, a knowing laugh
and a knowing wink. He spit again, a hard, straight jet, like

a blast from a well-primed squirt gun. This stain, an exclamation mark on the pure white snow, said how very well Clarence understood the Cobbs and their squabbles.

"Give us a bit more slack on your end," said George to Clarence. "We might want to raise the bucket and lift the whole rear end if it won't clear that tree coming out."

Clarence unwound the chain two turns and hooked it again. He stood aside squinting at the bus. "Judas, it's bright out here!" he said. Then he cast an eye on Jude. "That's not your name, is it?"

"Jude," said Jude, shaking his head.

"An important difference, I'd say," said Clarence with a grin, another wink, and another shot of tobacco juice. "I wouldn't want to be standing here with a Judas around."

Pulling was sufficient to free the bus without hitting the tree, and soon George drove it away with no more than an orange strip of its roof showing above the embankment and snow in cascades and clouds behind it.

Clarence stayed back, at George's direction, to plow open the Henley's driveway. With that job done, he drove down the road to do the same for Miss Thorpe's. Whatever George's thoughts about family coming first, he could be considerate in such ways. He liked doing favors for people, and he wasn't the sort to hang around for a thank you.

Clarence waved to Jude on his way back from Miss Thorpe's amid a vast roaring of the pea-green elephant bouncing along in high gear and a tobacco juice stain freezing on the door beneath his window.

After Jude had dug for an hour around their mailbox, he walked up the road a hundred yards to search for Harmon's. Poking his shovel handle into the snow embankment, he made a long row of holes where it ought to have been. He lowered the handle a foot and made a second row, with no more success. Then grabbing a low-hanging branch he pulled himself up on the embankment and walked along it. His boots tangled in the tops of chokecherry bushes while he ducked his head to miss tree limbs. He peered down into the dried ruins of a bird's nest where, incredibly, lay yet a whole, pale blue egg. He was examining this in the sunlight on his mitten palm when the snow gave way beneath him, and he sank to his arm pits with his legs straddling the very thing he'd been searching for. He never saw the pale blue egg again, but Harmon's mailbox surfaced with him as he raised himself up using oak limbs for hand holds. Inside it, none the worse for the box having been knocked from its post by the passing snowplow, he found *The Joys of Motherhood*, two weeks overdue and the real object of his search. He wedged Harmon's mailbox in a tree crotch and headed down the road the other way to the Woodcock.

Miss Thorpe's mailbox had escaped the general burial of things, but still he took a long time digging it out between glances up the hill to see if she might appear. Then there were more glances over his shoulder as he made his way back home without the conversation he'd hoped for.

17

More Misery than Joy

Next morning, he went to school with *The Joys of Motherhood* concealed in a large pocket of his winter coat. On his way to first hour class, he slipped into the library, empty save for Mr. Port who had his back to him while he tinkered with a projector on a push cart in the doorway of the audiovisual storeroom. Jude gingerly slid his book through a return slot beneath the checkout desk, took a second to enjoy the relief he felt, and then greeted Mr. Port.

"Oh, good morning, Jude," said the librarian straightening up and turning around. While adjusting his glasses which were lying cockeyed on his nose, he said, "Am I glad to see you!"

"You are?" Jude backed toward the door. Since he'd already returned *Robinson Crusoe* and *George Washington*, he feared from the look of him that Mr. Port had *The Joys of Motherhood* on his mind.

"My student assistant typed up the overdue book list yesterday afternoon ..."

"She did?" Jude backed further away. His blue eyes opened very wide for this early in the day.

"... and she's tacking up copies on the school bulletin boards this very minute."

A lump formed in Jude's throat, a large breath-constricting lump, a lump that felt as big as a book lodged there.

"And wouldn't you know it, but just this minute I'm told that Miss Greshmer needs a projector in her art room. That's on one end of the building, and on the other end, second floor, I'm supposed to deliver another projector to Mr. Evanson's consumer math class. Then I have to be back here in five minutes for a study hall. It can't be done without help, Jude. Do you think you could wheel this one down to the art room?"

Jude said he could do that, and as he was taking the cart from Mr. Port, he managed to ask about the overdue book list.

"Mandy Gordon worked on it yesterday afternoon; it's quite a long list this time."

"Mandy!"

"She's my assistant this quarter."

"Uh—I was absent yesterday. The busses weren't running, you know. I had an overdue book—it's there now." Jude pointed to the return slot.

"Well, don't worry about it. As long as they come back in a reasonable time, I don't mind." Mr. Port yanked an overhead projector from the lower shelf of the pushcart and hurried past Jude out the door. "Don't forget—Miss Greshmer's," he said without looking back. "Thanks, Jude."

His way to the art room took him past the main office bulletin board and Mandy Gordon who was just putting up a copy of the overdue book list. Jude peered over her shoulder and immediately found his name alongside *The Joys of Motherhood*.

"Hi, Mandy." Trying his best to sound nonchalant, he could manage only a squeak. He reached over her shoulder with a pen. "I returned my book just now, so we can cross out my name."

"You keep your hands off this list, Jude Henley!" Mandy wheeled around and shielded the list behind her back.

"But my book is in," said Jude.

"Your baby is two weeks past due," squealed Mandy. She patted his coat front. "I'm really surprised that it doesn't show more."

"Is that my projector?" shouted Miss Greshmer from the art room doorway. She tramped towards them on platform shoes.

"It's yours," Jude said. "I brought it for Mr. Port."

"Thanks heaps," said Miss Greshmer from beneath her acne, "but where is the power cord?"

"It's there," said Mandy. She pointed to the lower shelf of the cart. She hadn't moved away from the bulletin board.

"Thanks heaps," said Miss Greshmer pushing the cart away.

"Jude Henley, I'll scream, so help me, I will."

"I've already talked to Mr. Port about it—he knows my book is in."

"I'll scream if you lay a hand on this list—there's Mr. Willoughby looking at us now."

Desmond Willoughby, Principal of Twin Rivers High, could appear to be the most languid soul on the face of the earth. His placid surface, however, lay like poorly reinforced concrete heaved and cracked over a bad case of nerves, his placidity not that of a man at ease, but of a man in perpetual shock. His was the torpor of emotions long ago spent, leaving in their wake a vacuum. It was the contrived calm of one who struggled to control an ulcer, who tried lowering his blood pressure by sitting heavily upon it and, of course, crossing his legs. On Mr. Willoughby's desk, a bottle of milky stomach antacid was stuck, glued there by the last of a hundred dribbles dribbling down after furtive gulps and drying on its sides in knobby cascades like wax on a burnt-out candle.

At the moment Mandy noticed him in the rumpled brown suit that almost all older principals wear, he was wearily studying her and Jude from behind the glass wall of the Twin Rivers High administrative offices. Jude waved to him casually and strolled away to his class. Mr. Willoughby didn't wave back. He didn't nod or smile. He lowered his eyelids a fraction, as if adjusting the shades of a window.

That afternoon in geometry class Peter Johnson had a question for Jude as they brushed past each other on their way to their desks. He wanted to know Jude's opinion of breast feeding.

"Tell me on the bus tonight," he cackled. Then, as if protecting his nose, he raised a forearm across his face and ducked away.

18

Seeing All Sides

Jude didn't take the bus home. Feeling as though he couldn't face Peter or anybody else, not even Phyllis, he walked downtown after school instead. Gutters were awash with melting snow, a brown, tacky mire sucking at his boots. Something similar sucked at his brain as he tramped along with the notion of walking out to the highway and hitchhiking home. He'd never done this before, so mixed in with his gloom over the day's embarrassment was the thrill of adventure. Gloom lay in his brain, adventure in the pit of his stomach.

Plowed snow obstructed his passage at most intersections. He had an illusion of climbing up and down endless flights of stairs as he traversed these gray, slushy piles. With the afternoon ending, Twin Rivers work crews were busy launching the Christmas shopping season. At several main crossings, men stood on truck ladders working over the tops of traffic signals to string across the street plastic evergreen garland and chains of silver bells. Their voices echoed down the streets as they shouted directions to one another. Carols rang from many store entrances. A bell tinkled from a plywood kiosk where an overweight man tended a charity pot. Jude wasn't in the mood for any of it.

Beyond the shopping district, he passed through something that fit better, a bleaker and forlorn section of Twin

Rivers, a neighborhood of taverns, dingy cafes, and businesses which seemed in various stages of bankruptcy behind facades of chipped paint and dirty plate glass. A spotted mongrel bounded from an alley and frisked after him, alternately sniffing his tracks and veering away to sniff street signposts, fire hydrants, and car tires. From another alley, a garbage truck trash compactor moaned and howled. A baby cried in an apartment over one of the dingy cafes; pins fell in a bowling alley when a door opened, and silence descended again when it closed. Another door exhaled smoke, mildew, and a staggering man who squinted against what was left of the brilliant afternoon as he draped his arm over the shoulders of a woman taller by a head than he.

"Helen," the man sighed.

"God!" the woman said.

Jude hurried by but glanced back to see them tottering in tandem down the street away from him with the mongrel at *their* heels now. It was only then that he noticed they had come from *Dwyer's Purple Palace* whose purple canvas marquee extended across the sidewalk to the curb. He had walked right under it without noticing. As far as he could see, it was the only thing purple about the Purple Palace, not in the least like a palace. Above it soared a neon sign, morose in daylight, a faded, extinguished coil dripping snow, but by night a colored water fountain, and the first of many things about the Purple Palace that looked better at night than by light of day.

A block away, from the highway shoulder, Jude stuck out his thumb, a hesitating first gesture in the direction of his independence, and George Cobb pulled over as if waiting right there to pick him up.

"Don't you like my wife's driving?" asked George.

"I didn't feel like riding the bus tonight—are you heading home by any chance?"

"You bet," said George, with gin on his breath, "and we'll beat her damned old bus any day." He hit a button on his car radio, and from sets of stereo speakers front and rear came sounds of a rosary recited, *The Lord's Prayer* and *Hail Marys* led by a lone man and answered by a murmuring crowd.

"I just saw you walking away from the Purple Palace," said George. "You didn't stop in for a look at Buster, did you?"

"I didn't even know what it was till after I walked by it. Anyway, they'd kick me out since I'm not of age, and my mom would have a fit if she found out."

"Your mom is a nice woman, a hard-working, sensible woman," drawled George. "You're lucky to have a mom like that." Then he laughed because Jude's age suddenly struck him as a very amusing thought. "But you'll have a look in the Purple Palace sometime, no matter what she or anybody thinks. I'm not encouraging it, mind you, but I'm saying that it's bound to happen. Do you know what I mean?"

"I'm not sure."

"I mean it's all part of growing up, feeling that you have to see all sides, the good and the bad, even if it bothers people who care about you. But you would have missed Buster just now—her show doesn't start till later on. I was just in there myself, and it's quiet as a church inside. Funny thing sometimes how much a nightclub with nothing much going on can seem like a church. People even talk in hushed tones."

Holy Mary, mother of God, pray for us sinners ...

"You probably wonder why I'm listening to this," said George. "It's the same thing for me every day at this time—I have a drink in Twin Rivers or wherever the closest bar is, and I drive home listening to the rosary on my radio. I'm not a Catholic, but it's relaxing—all those people saying the same things over and over. After a drink or two, I'll take it over music any time. Do you know what I mean?"

"I'm not sure," said Jude again.

"Seeing all sides, living all sides—booze, Buster, and prayers..." George hesitated as if he found himself on the verge of a thought too profound for words.

Pray for us sinners, now and at the hour of our death. Amen.

"Do you know why they call her Buster?"

"I guess I can imagine."

"Boobs," said George not willing to take any chances on Jude's imagination.

Holy Mary ...

"Oh," said Jude.

"The damnedest set you'll ever see."

Beyond the second bridge over the North Crow River, where the Twin Rivers highway makes a broad curve climbing into some wooded hills, George pulled out to pass a string of cars and Phyllis's bus at the head of them. Conspicuous in the rear of the bus were Peter Johnson and Ronny Faber looking out at traffic in their trail. Jude bent low pretending to search for something on the floor as George hit the accelerator.

The Third Sorrowful Mystery, The Crowning with Thorns.

George had passed three cars and was pulling even with the bus. Straightening up, Jude caught a glimpse of Phyllis' baseball cap, a slash of blue sky, and then much more than a glimpse of a gasoline transport truck bearing down on them. It veered toward the shoulder with its chrome air horns blasting. For an instant, it appeared to fill up the entire universe in front of them. Then George cut in front of the bus with little more than a car length to spare. Behind him Phyllis honked and flashed her lights.

"Not even close," muttered George. "What's wrong with that truck driver anyway, trying to make it look closer than it was? Boy will I catch hell about this from my old lady."

Jude stared straight ahead down the highway at the center lines rushing toward them. They were doing ninety-five. He thought he should say something, not about their speed, but about their near head-on collision. He ought to have agreed with George that it hadn't been close, and he felt George beside him waiting for it. Agreeability was expected because George was doing him a favor, agreeability even if Jude's thumping heart couldn't agree. Even so this was George, he thought, and he could go on being honest, even when it wasn't honesty George wanted at the moment. He thought their habit of honesty with each other was too important to break for any reason, so he said. "It was real close, George."

"Yeah, I guess so," George admitted as if he expected Jude to say this and was ready to agree.

"I felt it in the pit of my stomach."

Holy Mary, mother of God, pray for us sinners, now and at the hour of our death. Amen.

"That's another thing I like about listening to the rosary," said George. "It reminds me of things I need to think about more than I do."

A few minutes passed with George silent, but Jude could tell he was thinking hard about something. He started talking again as Twisters hove into view ahead of them.

"I was sitting at the Palace bar with half a martini left, when somebody went out, and through the open door I saw you walking by, Jude. I left my martini and came to give you a ride. I said to myself, there goes Jude Henley. There goes one person I can talk to. Life sure is funny," said George, "all sides of it."

Jude was left off at the sandy road. He stood around in front of Twisters Café till the bus came by. He wanted Phyllis, who might not have noticed him in her husband's car, to see that he got home all right. Otherwise she'd fret his mother about it later on. Phyllis coasted by with her window open.

"I told you some weird type would pick you up if you tried hitchhiking home," she shouted.

Jude waved and turned away before he had to see Peter and Ronny. Ahead of him, the sandy road had become a blue tunnel of shadowy snow blazing with sunset on the embankment top. Also ahead of him were all the cabin roofs he meant to sweep before supper using Harmon's long-handled broom. And also ahead was the event he hoped to avoid witnessing, this being the day, the very hour next, that Miss Thorpe had picked to move out of Hawkers Park. He wasn't thinking about any of this at the moment though. *George isn't weird; Miss Thorpe isn't weird; I'm not weird.*

THE FAR END OF THE PARK

He stooped to pull at a stick protruding from what was left of snow on the roadside. As his luck would have it, the stick came out free of anything larger. In his hand, it became a weapon of choice hurled through the air with the deftness and certainty of a thrower of javelins. It did not behave in the least like a javelin however. It spun like a boomerang before striking the heart of an imagined target. As happens in tournaments and in life, the conclusion of one event led to another regardless.

19

Lights Out, Lights On

Had George driven the speed limit that afternoon, Jude wouldn't have seen Miss Thorpe leave. He'd come slowly down through the park engrossed in the task of clearing each roof, a job complicated by the day's thawing and then its re-freezing to form an icy crust over the remaining snow. Yet despite this new difficulty, it felt good to be alone with his thoughts and a job he could throw himself into, to be away from anyone he felt compelled to fight with or agree with. He took his time. Before he'd finished with cabin eleven, the sky was black with the faintest of stars twinkling in it.

His eyes wandered among these while his broom handle hung from an eave. As he reached for it, the lights went out in cabin twelve above him on the hill. A door slammed, another opened with rusty protest, the dome light of Miss Thorpe's car revealed her in silhouette with what looked like a vase or a lamp and an armload of clothes she was packing into a back seat. She bent down and picked up a box which she slid into the front.

Jude turned away and ran home through the park. He ran by reflex, because he didn't want to see her go, not because he knew what he would do when he stopped running. The nearer he got to the Perch, the more *what to do* became a problem, and the slower he ran. He walked the last fifty yards and lingered outside on the step for a minute before going in. He brushed snow from his clothes and stomped his boots. Once inside he took a long time hanging up his coat.

"I guess there's something you ought to know," he said to his mother at last.

"And I guess there's something you ought to know," she replied, looking up from a stack of tool company flyers. "A letter came for you in the mail today." She pointed to the kitchen table where it lay, propped against a seashell, a pale blue envelope on the flap of which was written simply *Jeanne Thorpe* without a return address.

Inside Jude found this written on a sheet of pale blue stationery:

Thanks for lending a hand the other day. It was sure nice to have help when I really needed it. Maybe we'll run into each other again someday.

"Very thoughtful of her," said his mother when she heard. "Now what were you going to tell me?"

This made it even harder. He pretended to be engrossed in the letter. What do you say when the truth would only help someone who doesn't deserve it, and a lie might help someone who does? He knew his mother could never lie to Harmon. If she knew it, she would have to tell him, but she wouldn't enjoy hurting Miss Thorpe either, so a lie here would also make her life a little easier. Later on, when Harmon returned and found out for himself, Jude would be the only one to blame. Months would have passed, Miss Thorpe might be working again, and his mother would be out of it.

"Jude?" she asked him again. "What on earth is troubling you tonight?"

He swallowed hard and revealed something he hadn't intended telling her, though she seemed likely to hear it from Phyllis. He told her about hitchhiking home and catching a ride with George. Of course, this forced him to explain why he hadn't ridden the bus. Even if it made little sense without the details of *The Joys of Motherhood* and Mandy's overdue booklist, he had to tell it that way. This earned him a puzzled look, but he changed the subject before she could ask any questions and helped her clear the table for supper.

"I swept all the cabin roofs tonight," he said.

"So that's why your clothes are so wet. I thought maybe you stayed off the bus because you'd gotten in a snowball fight after school."

Between his potatoes and a piece of fish he paused for the usual inquiry about Miss Thorpe. When it didn't come, as if she too had begun to avoid that subject, he felt he had to go ahead regardless. If he had to think any more about deceiving her, he knew he'd never do it, so he said straight out that Miss Thorpe was singing as usual, and for good measure he added that tonight she'd been singing Christmas carols.

"I wish I could have heard them," she said.

And it pained him that he had gone so far in deceiving her.

Their conversation that evening never turned back to Miss Thorpe. When it was snow on the cabin roofs instead and how he managed sweeping them off, she didn't ask about Miss Thorpe's roof. When it was Christmas plans, brought on by his mention of carols, she didn't ask what carols he heard her sing. Finally, supper was behind them, the dishes were done, his homework beckoned as seldom before. With what seemed the hardest part over now, Jude thought he could keep it up till Miss Thorpe was away so long that Harmon would never catch her and make her pay, and even if he did finally catch her, at least they wouldn't have been involved in it.

Her cabin was dark the night through though. If possible, something had to be done about that since lights had become their beacon assuring them that she was there yet. They never stepped outside after dark without looking for a light from some window on the distant hilltop.

Next day in a study hall with Mr. Port presiding, Jude's eyes wandered from a book he wasn't reading to the library windows. Outside across the street in a school parking lot, Mr. Willoughby had just pulled into the space reserved for his car. It had been a day of fog created by the warming temperatures and melting snow. Mr. Willoughby walked away with his car lights still on. A ringing bell ended study hall. Thirty books slammed shut, thirty chairs slid back from tables, twenty-nine voices could be heard at once. Jude, silent, searched for a plan.

"Please," shouted Mr. Port to the twenty-nine talkers, "wait till you're out in the hallway. Please."

On the way to his next class, Jude entered the administrative suite. "Tell Mr. Willoughby he left his car lights on," he said to a secretary. He was on his way back out when Mr. Willoughby himself called to him from the doorway of his office.

"Wait a second, Jude," he said, stepping out and handing him a set of car keys. "Would you mind going out and shutting them off for me? I'm in the middle of a meeting."

Perhaps because he was in the middle of something, Mr. Willoughby was unusually brisk.

"No problem," said Jude, "But I might be late for my next class."

"My secretary will write you a pass," said Mr. Willoughby.

"Thanks a lot. My battery would have been dead, and tonight is my wedding anniversary. We need more kids like you in this school."

Later on, had he been able to look closely at all that had happened since the school year began, Jude might have seen this moment as a turning point, the instant his string of bad turns ended with a sharp good turn. Mr. Willoughby's battery didn't die that day; his secretary beamed at Jude when he returned his car keys; his late pass for Mr. Evanson's geometry class said, *Running an important errand for the Principal*, enough to turn Mr. Evanson's frown into a congenial smile; and most of all—yes most of all—because Mr. Willoughby had both left his lights on and forgotten to lock his car, Jude now had a plan. Only a bit of luck was needed.

After a bus ride home, during which Peter and Ronny had been unusually subdued, Jude set out from Twisters with the early darkness of the first day of December settling in. He stopped by the Perch, where his mother wasn't home yet, picked up a flashlight, and headed straight to the far end of the park. Along his way, he retrieved the long-handled broom from the eave of the cabin nearest the Woodcock. From there he walked straight up the driveway to a door he had never dared approach before.

He gave its latch a tentative twist, and then stepped back for a few seconds, dismayed. Miss Thorpe had locked the door, the bad luck he didn't need. He kicked his way around the Woodcock in snow still knee deep. Its windows were also locked. He headed back down the driveway. If he hadn't slipped and dropped his flashlight in the snow a second later, if he had worn gloves this evening, if not all of this, his plan might have remained as defeated as it seemed a moment before. Instead he retrieved the flashlight from the snow, and then shoved his bare hand into his pocket to warm it. His fingers tangled in the Perch's key. Seconds later he was standing in the open doorway of what only yesterday had been Miss Thorpe's cabin.

Here was another unlooked-for way all the cabins were alike: the same key fit all their doors. Instead of buying new locks every time a tourist lost his key or went home with a key forgotten in his pocket, instead of trying to keep track of eleven keys and locks, Harmon made copies of a master key to fit them all and left the Pike's key out of it. Only he would be the wiser, and if anyone did figure it out, what difference would it make? Here was another moment he might have looked in a mirror and smiled at himself, at least until today when it made all the difference. Jude's desperate last shot had hit its mark.

Soon he found the courage to direct his flashlight around the room. She had been able to lock the door from the inside on her way out. Her brass key lay on a kitchen table much like their table, with two chairs instead of the three they had. Near the kitchen sink was a coffee can with something, maybe a rag, hanging out of it. With the door opened a little wider, his light found a chair and couch that seemed as shapeless as theirs, a heater with no flame dancing in its window, his breath in a cold room, and something new to concern him.

He already knew the cabins were identical. Miss Thorpe's, much as its exterior differed from the others, was identical within. He didn't have to look or step inside. He could reach left around the door frame to find her main light switch precisely where the Perch's was. He flicked it on, shut the door, locked it again, and quickly turned away.

He needed to do two further things. First, he found the valve to her water line behind the cabin where he used to sit listening to her songs. She had turned it off already and drained the pipes from a spigot left open there, just as he had seen Harmon do when he closed up the resort last fall. So there would be no burst water pipes, no damage of that sort to blame her for, and no unpaid fuel oil bill with the heat turned off. Then he swept the Woodcock's roof. He took even more time than he had with the others. Everything about this had to be done right.

Under this roof, with its snow now coming off in a series of small avalanches, her life must have been much the same as theirs on the other end of the park. To know this, he didn't have to see more than the wandering beam of his flashlight had shown him as he stood a few seconds trembling in her doorway. He stretched to reach the higher points above him, to sweep everything clean. Snow avalanches made soft plopping sounds all around him. And though she might never find out what a good friend he had been and was still trying to be, he thought he had to try, regardless *he had to try*.

20

Getting it Straight

April came, the off-season in Hawkers Park neared its end, and Jude, glancing out one Saturday morning, discovered Harmon Grove's green and white van parked so precisely in its old place alongside the Pike that it seemed never to have been anywhere else.

The first thing Harmon wanted to know was why his mailbox was wedged ten feet up in the crotch of an oak. Next, he positively demanded to know when Miss Thorpe had moved out and why he hadn't been told. This question so surprised Jude's mother, and she seemed so genuinely unable to answer even Harmon had to believe she knew nothing about it.

"We could see her light on every night," she told him.

After Harmon stormed out, slamming the door behind him, she turned to Jude. "You told me you heard her singing up there, but he says she's been gone for months as far as he can tell."

"I thought I could hear her," Jude said, wincing from the reproach in her voice, but at least this was the truth, for after she left he had sometimes gone up there, and whether because he recalled it so vividly or because of a trick of the wind, he actually thought he could hear her singing yet. "Maybe it was just my imagination," he admitted.

"Or your sense of justice," she replied, not angrily. "Tell me the truth, Jude—there's no point in keeping your secret any longer."

Jude by this time had sunk himself into the sagging chair, folded his arms, and was staring at the toes of his shoes. "I thought she needed our help," he said. "She knew all along that we were working for Harmon."

"Which we were *supposed* to be doing, you might have recalled."

"Miss Thorpe thought I was spying on her."

"And wasn't that one of our jobs?"

Jude curled even deeper into the chair, avoiding her gaze, which wasn't faraway this time, but was fixed directly upon him.

"Miss Thorpe didn't have any money. Her cabin would have been empty all winter anyway. Why should people like Harmon have everything their way?"

"That's not the point—it's a matter of responsibility and honoring the commitments you make to people. The fact that you happen to like someone or not to like someone else doesn't really matter. Besides, you might know enough about Harmon not to like him, but how much do you know about Miss Thorpe? Not much, certainly, having met her just once. I'm sure you imagine her to be much more help- less than she is. She's probably more capable and tougher than Harmon—in her line of work, she'd have to be both. You call her *Miss Thorpe* all the time because we got started doing that last fall, but I'll bet she's hardly ever been called that in her whole life. She'd probably laugh in your face if you called her Miss Thorpe. That's how much you know about her, Jude, not enough to be taking sides."

He wished the sagging chair would swallow him whole and then spend a year digesting him.

"Maybe so," he responded feebly when she seemed to be waiting for his response.

"So let's at least get your motives straight in our own minds since Harmon will think what he wants regardless. You stuck up for her because you thought it was the fair thing and because you don't like our landlord, and you would take almost anyone's side against a man like that."

"I guess so," he said, but he thought maybe it was more complicated. Was taking Miss Thorpe's side the same as taking *anyone's* side? Everything seemed like guesswork, like what you did when you came to a multiple-choice question you couldn't answer in school. It seemed better to guess than leave it blank. You just picked out something and hoped it was right. People like Harmon made it easier. You would never guess *Harmon* when *Miss Thorpe* was another choice. She wasn't just *anybody*.

Then as suddenly as she had come at him to find out the truth, his mother relented, her voice softened to its usual tone, her eyes began to take on that faraway look. "It's pretty much what your father would have done," she said.

Jude couldn't imagine him at all, not even a guess. He could never have explained himself by saying he was just like his father.

"But why did you lie to me all these months?"

"I'm sorry," he said.

She bent over to kiss him on the forehead, and when he climbed up out of the chair, she kissed him again, standing on her tiptoes because he'd grown that much over the fall and winter. She turned away, then, and said nothing more about it, but he knew it was all right between them now. She had forgiven him. That much at least wasn't a guess.

21

Having it Out

In the weeks before tourists once again filled Hawkers Park, Harmon busied himself preparing for them while Jude busied himself avoiding Harmon who seemed always to have in his hands a step ladder, hammer, or paint brush, and for Jude a thick look of rebuke, so far silent. Jude didn't expect it to remain so. He knew that soon enough Harmon would have plenty to say to him about Miss Thorpe, and in the meantime, almost harder to endure was his critical glare and (if he could get close enough to Jude) his scolding tone, even if he spoke only of the weather and how dry a spring this was.

Jude felt lucky to be away in school much of the time. His problems there had vanished over the winter. At least as he saw it, he'd found his way back into the middle of the pack again, unnoticed and happy to be there. After school and on weekends he did his best to keep out of Harmon's way, but with the two of them and his mother still having the park to themselves, this wasn't easy.

He and Harmon seemed to be alone in a small boat far out on the sea. Neither of them could make a move without bumping into the other. Moreover, Harmon's aim was the opposite of Jude's, for he wanted it that way. Whatever end of the park he worked, Jude tried to be on the other, but first chance, if he didn't look out, Harmon would move and be working near him, as close as he could get. Any excuse served him to step on Jude's heels and breathe down his neck with his doggy breath. He seemed to wash windows he had already washed the day before and hammer at a rain gutter that wouldn't have come loose in a hundred wind-storms. Had Jude gone completely out of the park, out into the meadow across the sandy road, Harmon appeared ready to slink after him, trimming trees that weren't even his, repairing fences around fields he didn't own.

One afternoon, Jude's desperation sent him up to Twisters Café to try his luck with pinball again. Even the skinny man's company was better than this. He hadn't been there ten minutes; he hadn't lost a dollar yet, when he heard Harmon's voice behind him and turned to see him sitting at the mostly empty lunch counter visiting with the skinny man. Jude soon found this 'silent treatment' more of an ordeal than anything he had gone through at school. It wore him out and made him dread and hate weekends as much as he had once dreaded and hated school on days now well behind him.

It revived his old notion of getting books from the school library, though this time he was careful about titles. He would sit around the Perch reading them most evenings in-stead of going outside where Harmon was sure to be stalk-ing him in all weather. He actually read five books during the middle weeks of April and wrote a semester's worth of book reports for English. He studied so much that his im-proving grades threatened to put him on the honor roll. He was becoming almost the best student in geometry, all be-cause of Harmon prowling after him in the park and in his thoughts, peering at him between pages he read, poking his way into triangles where Jude himself and Miss Thorpe were the other points. Jude at last grew so tired of all this that he felt he must do something to end it, so one afternoon instead of reading or dodging away *he* followed Harmon for a change.

He had driven his van down the sandy road and up Miss Thorpe's driveway. Jude chased after him on the footpath above the ravine. Though he could distinctly hear water rippling far below him, newspapers reported that the North Crow was as low as it had ever been this time of spring. In a general science class, Jude's teacher had skipped a chapter on nutrition to study weather, especially the causes and effects of drought. The class had been cautioned about starting fires because forest fires were one effect. Grass stayed brown and shrubs were slow to leaf out—other effects. The woodlands and marshes were parched and as brown as last autumn in all but their wettest parts, but still Jude heard water running through Hawkers ravine, and still the deep, aromatic smells of spring decay floated up to him as he walked above it.

Hepaticas bloomed pink and bloodroot white alongside. A blue jay hopped ahead of him through the brush, reminding him of winter. Out in the park itself a dozen robins hopped from clump to clump. A flight of blackbirds swarmed out over the marshlands. After them came a heron with his long legs straight out behind him. Jude bent to pick a bloodroot whose red stem juice stained his fingers. He rubbed streaks of this aslant his cheek bones, painting his face as he had read of Indians doing long ago in these lands. It seemed to him a preparation for what lay directly ahead.

Harmon was painting Miss Thorpe's cabin. Jude, climb-ing toward it from the back of the hill, rehearsed a speech he imagined reciting in a minute or two. It began: *"All right, Mr. Grove, I've had about enough of this—now you listen here..."* It was a strong speech; an indignant, forth-right speech; a man-to-man speech which he would march right up to Harmon and deliver like a punch in the nose. But should he call him Mr. Grove or simply Harmon? Mr. Grove sounded too formal and Harmon too friendly. This requiring further thought, he settled down in the grass un-der the cabin window by the oil tank, his old place where the sod still appeared flattened from all his sitting there the autumn before.

Perhaps the familiar comfort he found there brought back the easy feeling of an earlier time when he sat there alone—or almost alone. It wasn't long before having it out with Harmon looked like a really stupid idea. He lost track of any reason for being there. He leaned back with his head against the wall—just as he used to—forgot about Harmon working only a few feet away, and instead half expected to hear Miss Thorpe singing once more. His eyes even closed for a moment.

His head happened to be resting against the very wall Harmon was inside painting just then, behind the gas range where he was having a hard time on account of the close quarters, and so his brush handle struck the copper tubing running outside to a small propane tank an inch to the left of Jude's head. An explosive vibration hummed though the tank and settled in Jude's spine. He rolled away, alarmed, and when he jumped up to run, his eyes came level with the back window and its blue curtain shoved aside revealing the dark, critical gaze of Harmon peering out at him. The window sash flew open with a bang, and Harmon shouted through the screen.

"What are you doing hanging around back here?"

"I ... I was wondering if you needed any help." This was the first thing Jude could think of to say, also the most stupid and the least believable. Completely forgotten was a speech beginning, *"All right, Mr. Grove ... would you rather be called Mr. Grove or just plain Harmon?"*

Just plain Harmon said, "I might need help, but you're the last person I'd expect to get it from. Snooping is what I think you were doing here. Well, you should have snooped more last winter, my boy. This Thorpe woman was out of here at least three months, and you didn't even figure that out. Do you know why?"

Jude shook his head so hard that his hair flew into his eyes. He backed further away from the window. The shiny black bill of Harmon's nautical cap tilted down, pointing straight at his heart.

"I'll tell you why," Harmon continued. "Thorpe was clever, and you were dumb and lazy." He gestured toward the ceiling light Jude had left on last winter, a yellow bulb burning in a bare porcelain socket. He squinted slyly at it as if it had shared a secret Jude was too stupid to know. "She left this light on," he said "—and that was pretty clever—so dumb, lazy people like you would think she still lived here, unless they did what they were told and walked all the way up here to have a closer look. But you didn't do that, did you?"

Jude shook his head again, first yes, then no.

Harmon fumed on non-stop. "You didn't come here and notice that there weren't tracks in the fresh snow. You didn't look for her car or listen for sounds. You were dumb and lazy, so you didn't catch her, and we couldn't call the sheriff right away, could we?"

"No, sir," Jude said, relaxing a little somewhere between being scared and being relieved now that it was clear how completely Harmon had been fooled. Harmon's anger scared him, but the man was also saying some of the most ridiculous things he'd ever heard.

"What's that all over your face?"

"Bloodroot."

"Bloodroot? You look like the devil himself, I'd say, and it doesn't surprise me any. No, my boy, I'm not surprised to catch you snooping around here when it's too late to do any good. I've been keeping a close eye on you lately, and you're a *lurker*. Do you know what a lurker is?"

"No, sir."

"A lurker is someone who hangs around with his hands in his pockets. He doesn't do anything. He has no sense of direction, no place to go, so he just lurks. He doesn't know what else to do with himself. It all comes of growing up without a father if you ask me." Harmon paused and glanced up at the light again. "Thorpe was clever all right," he said, changing the subject, "and she was lucky too. This light bulb burnt the whole time till I got back from Florida. If it had burnt out, even you might have caught her, right?"

"I guess so," said Jude.

"And this same bulb still works—imagine that!" Again, Harmon glanced over his shoulder. He had mixed feelings about this bulb. A man owning twelve light-bulb-gobbling cabins could admire one that refused to be gobbled. He could also resent it as a bit of bad luck costing him five hundred times what it saved him.

Jude was happy not to inform him that twice over the winter when the bulb had burnt out, he had gone into the Woodcock to replace it with another he'd found in the storage building, and that he'd been able to let himself in with a key Harmon provided. He had taken a further step back from the window, while Harmon looked away.

"—Where are you sneaking off to now? If you've come here to help me, which I don't believe at all, then get in here and help. I'll make an honest man of you yet."

So Harmon and Jude at last had it out, though far from the way Jude rehearsed. Even farther from his thinking was the result that he should be spending the rest of the afternoon working for him, following Harmon's paint brush with a rag and a can of thinner, cleaning from baseboards and floor drops of paint he spilled. Harmon painted with a roller and then with a brush near windows and doors. Either way he was sloppy, perhaps because it was his nature, perhaps because he relished making work for Jude. Regardless, Jude must have erased a thousand drops.

Two hours passed before Harmon stood up from low in a corner where the last patch of beige wall had disappeared beneath what the paint can label called *Trembling Fern Green*. He stepped into the center of the room to admire his work while Jude mopped up the last of the spots behind him. Miss Thorpe was really gone from the Woodcock now, every last sign of her, to his relief, swept out clean and painted over with *Trembling Fern*, which for all the lightness suggested by its name, was a deep-toned, murky hue, more monster-green than ferny.

"That does it for this job," said Harmon. "Now give me a hand moving the range back." He was strong enough to move two such ranges by himself, one stacked atop the other, but he had discovered the pleasure of ordering Jude around.

Jude got up from the corner where he had finished with the last of Harmon's carelessness. They nudged the heavy range inch by inch into its old place against the wall, and Harmon sprawled on the floor behind it to reconnect the copper tubing. It jerked in the wall again. Outside the gas tank rang again.

"Go out and open the gas valve," grunted Harmon from behind the range. "Shout when you've done it."

When Jude shouted, Harmon raised the black burner grills and lit the pilot light. After that, he lit each of its four burners. Each hissed a second then flared with a popping sound, like a rug when it's shaken outside, which was something else they did before the afternoon ended. Harmon turned all the burners as high as they would go, till their flaming circles lengthened into orange cones before collapsing with a sigh and a farewell pop as he turned each off. When he opened the oven to light that also, he discovered a white casserole dish. He tossed it into a box of trash where it struck an empty paint can and shattered.

"It must have been hers," he said. "I don't want anything that's hers. Too bad it wasn't worth much though." He stood facing Jude with his hands on his hips, a sort of wrestler pose, with his tee shirt blotchy with Trembling Fern, more stained than even the rag hanging from Jude's belt. Harmon's arms were green to his elbows, his face a case of green measles. He looked triumphant. "So the range works, and this room is all painted," he said, "… except for the closet. Damn it, I forgot the closet, and we don't have time to do it today."

Jude didn't like the way he said we. It suggested more days like this one. He began to wonder what spring activities might still be available for him to join after school. Track—maybe it wasn't too late to go out for track.

Harmon had thrown open the closet door and shoved a cluster of hangers jangling to one end of a clothes bar. The closet walls were the same beige he had eclipsed everywhere else. "I guess this is hers, too," he said, pulling a blue windbreaker jacket from a hook behind the door and flinging it toward his trash box. "If she had to sneak out, why didn't she at least take all her crap with her instead of leaving it for me to clean up? I don't want anything that's hers."

Jude wasn't listening. Having fallen short of the box, the jacket lay in a heap at his feet where a silver cross and chain slid from one of its pockets. While Harmon raved like a movie monster, Jude bent to pick up the cross, and now he held it dangling from its chain, glinting and dancing beneath the 'indestructible' ceiling bulb. He seemed to be holding Miss Thorpe in his fingers—the last of her in Hawkers Park—in this ornately cut cross whose whitened silver and faintly fractured turquoise insets showed it to be far more ancient than its chain. Then Harmon jerked it away.

"What do we have here?" he chortled. "Aha aha ha! Look what we have." This time we didn't seem to include Jude.

"It's hers," said Jude.

"Not anymore, my boy."

"You said you didn't want anything of hers."

"I was talking about her crap," said Harmon grinning all over, "but this, I want—this I definitely want. This is a horse of a different feather." He twirled the cross from its chain. It whirled in circles around his index finger.

"You aren't really going to keep it, are you?"

"Why not?"

"It's hers—it doesn't belong to you." Jude, earlier in the afternoon unable to argue on his own behalf, now had much to say.

"It's sterling," said Harmon. He was too preoccupied to notice the boy he thought of as a punk, a lurker and a punk, had dared argue with him. "It isn't worth a lot, but still it's worth something. Who knows? It might have great sentimental value, perhaps a gift from a deceased mother, or an inheritance from a grandmother. It might be important enough to her that she'll pay up what she owes to get it back. So I'm holding it for ransom, let's say, not keeping it, just holding it. Think of it that way if you're so bothered— not that I care a feather what you think." He waved Jude outside. The cross and chain had disappeared into his pants pocket. "I want you to help me again tomorrow after school. When do you get home?"

"I ... I don't think I like it," Jude said, hard as it was to say with Harmon standing close enough to strike him.

"You don't like what?"

"Working for you."

"Working for me? Why, you punk!" Harmon roared. "You'll work for me when I want, or I'll send you and your mother packing to hell out of my park."

THE FAR END OF THE PARK

They faced each other by the side of Harmon's van, the burly retired wrestler painted all over, the suddenly lanky boy nearly his height. Catkins from late-leafing aspens dropped around them in golden, pollen-laden tangles. One brushed Jude's cheek in falling—a gentle touch—as if an angel's wing hovering to rest itself upon his folded arms. He gazed at it, so distressed that he hardly recognized what it was, swallowing his anger—surprised that there could be so much of it and that it unleashed so much strength—swallowing his pride and his sense of justice, swallowing everything for the sake of the shabby life he and his mother were given here in Hawkers Park.

"I'm sorry," he said after what seemed a long time, but had been seconds merely. "I didn't mean it that way."

"Don't tell me what you mean," bellowed Harmon. "I have ears." One of Harmon's ears was mostly Trembling Fern.

"I get home about four o'clock."

"That's better. That's the way you answer me when I ask you something. That's what a father would have taught you. I'll make an honest man of you yet, and next time don't show up with your face painted like a savage."

Harmon gave him a paint-splattered smirk, with his monster-green arms folded across his paint-smeared shirt over his heart which the world already knew to be a monstrously large heart.

"Tomorrow we're going to start a fire," he said as he climbed into his van. "I'll see you at four."

22

Burning Breeches

Only when he spoke of setting fire to it did Jude learn that Harmon's property included a hundred acres of the wild river grasslands he had so often gazed upon from Miss Thorpe's hill. His part of the marsh lay immediately beyond the ravine, a sedgy, tear-shaped expanse whose natural border was the meandering North Crow on one side and on the other side the eastern ridge of a Christmas tree farm owned by the families of Peter Johnson and Ronny Faber. Harmon planned to start his fire below the tree farm along a margin of willow brush, with the wind blowing out and away towards the river. It would extinguish itself at the water's edge, and last summer's dead grasses would be cleared to make room for the season's new growth.

He hailed Jude from the backyard of the Pike as he was coming home from school. His eyes had a nearly jovial twinkle, as if his childish delight in the fire he was about to start had already burnt away yesterday's bad feelings toward the boy.

"Well, let's do it," he said, dancing from one foot to the other. He pointed to the sky where a very few flat-topped white clouds glided along like fish in blue isolation. "This wind is the right wind. I got my burning permit from the state fire warden just after lunch. He's a friend of mine, you know, and he told me if I had waited another twenty-four hours, he wouldn't have been able to give me one. It's so dry that the state is about to ban even campfires, even smoking cigarettes outside. Boy am I glad I thought of burning off my slough before that happened." Harmon performed a sort of pirouette with a red gasoline can in his left hand.

His friend, the local fire warden, was the skinny man who ran Twisters Café, a warping, sun-bleached sign in the window of which usually said, *Burning Permits Here.* Across the highway, on the lawn of the white frame house where the skinny man lived, stood a redwood sign between a tall spruce tree and a wooden statue of Smokey Bear. This was something of a local tourist attraction with cars parking by it all summer long and people getting out to take pictures of their kids standing in front of Smokey. Smokey's left arm pivoted, his gloved fingers pointing toward words on the redwood sign, Forestry Department words for fire conditions in the area woods. Much of early winter, Smokey had seemed frozen in a snow drift up to his waist with his hand pointing to the words *wet* and *safe.* He changed his opinion to *normal* in January as the snow drift sank to his boot tops and finally melted away. By February already he pointed to *dry* and *caution advised.*

This afternoon, in getting off Phyllis's bus, Jude noticed the bear pointing to *severely dry* and *dangerous.* The only things higher on the redwood sign were *explosive* and a crow just then roosting on its very top. It was Jude's imagination, of course, but he thought Smokey's eyes were open wider than they'd usually been. A warm, dry wind had blown for another day, and had Jude turned around and walked back up to Twisters this very moment, he would have seen Smokey pointing to *explosive* now and the sign in the café just flipped around in the past fifteen minutes to say *No Burning Permits*.

"He thinks you're a punk," said Harmon of the skinny man as he and Jude stood together on the footpath and peered down into the cavernous ravine. "He says you need a father to set you straight, but I told him I could do the job anytime."

Bracing themselves against leaning basswood trees and grabbing handholds wherever they could find them in the brushy undergrowth, they worked their way down on the sides of their shoes. Gasoline sloshed around as Harmon shifted the can from one hand to another freeing whatever hand was nearest his next hold. "We could have driven in from the other side," he said, panting. "But this way is a lot closer."

As their difficulties increased, he ceased talking to Jude over his shoulder. Jude followed above him with a paper sack of rags Harmon had taken from his cabin, most of it his old socks and underwear. Far above them on the edge of the ravine, his green and white van stood parked in brilliant spring sunshine. Here in the cool, gloomy depths, with their descent at last ending on the river bank, Jude felt himself suddenly plunged in winter's leftover air, a dank mixture of decaying vegetation and the skinny man's bad opinion of his fatherless state. He shivered. How he hated being talked about, as if not having a father made him some sort of freak.

"Boy, oh boy, ain't this river low for the springtime though!" exclaimed Harmon with a flat, wheezing whistle.

"I've lived around here all my life and never seen it so low this time of year."

Jude shivered again.

The Thanksgiving weekend storm had provided the winter's only significant snow. He'd had to sweep the cabin roofs that one time only, and when most of the snow melted during a December and January of record warmth, the ground had been left bare to three months of drying winds with scarcely a morning fog to dampen it.

"We'll just follow the river now," said Harmon. Though he spoke softly, almost guiltily, his voice echoed from the ravine sides. He still panted from his climb down through the trees, but with two-thirds of the river bed dry and strewn with small, smooth stones, the rest of their way couldn't have been much easier if a road had been laid out for them by George Cobb's construction crew.

This was the kind of spring day to make the world seem like a room without furniture. The drifted snow is gone, trees and shrubs still mostly bare, the parched ground not very green with its very small plants, and so nothing much has hove in sight to replace what emptied out when winter left. Jude thought the blue sky seemed farther away than usual. Around them loomed this vast emptiness, especially down here in the ravine, along the course of a river that trickled when it should have been a flood, and which led like a roadway into the great arena of the wild marshes. Empty basswoods leaned overhead, shaggy vines hung like bell ropes without bells, and a lone hawk circling high above them was as solitary as the evening star. Everything emphasized emptiness, but nothing more than the silence of it all, so pronounced that the trickle of water over pebbles could be heard as distinctly as the patter of rain on their cabin roof in the middle of the night.

They followed the hawk out into sunshine on the point of the teardrop marsh. Once Harmon caught his breath, he became talkative again and seemed almost to be apologizing in advance for what he was about to do. He told Jude the price of hay, "even wild hay," was already high and would be higher than ever if the drought continued so long that alfalfa and clover crops were lost on the upland meadows. "But even in dry years this stuff will grow," he said waving his free hand over his acres in which scattered redwinged blackbirds perched like sentinels on last year's cattails. "I can sell all this for hay to one of the farmers around here. They'll be fighting over it, bidding the price up. Somehow I have to make up for my winter losses." He looked accusingly at Jude. "And since you had a hand in the losing, you ought to have a hand in the getting back." He licked a finger and stuck it up to test the wind. "Well, it ain't blowing as hard as it was an hour ago, but it's still heading east straight towards the river."

"What if it starts blowing some other way?" Jude dared ask with his eyes exploring the willow copse in which they had paused. Trees and shrubs there were as dry as dead sticks which somehow managed to swell and pop their furry buds regardless. Nearby, looking little better off than Christmas trees that had been cut and used and left to wilt in garbage dumps, were the long-needled pines of the Johnson and Faber Tree Farm.

"Listen here," said Harmon, perturbed and suddenly back in his old hectoring mood, "you mouth off a lot because you never had a father to shut you up. If you knew what *I* did, you'd be certain that the wind, if it does anything at all on a day like this, just dies out at sunset. It *won't* start blowing another way." He paused to perform a kind of mocking jig with the gas can in one hand and a pair of torn undershorts in the other. "What kind of a turkey-brain do you take me for anyway? Do you think I'd set a match to all this if I had any doubt about which way the wind would blow? Why, half the county could go up in flames."

Jude wouldn't have risked telling Harmon what he thought of his brain, but for a second, as he heard him out, he seemed to feel a slight gust against his other cheek.

"I've been burning off this marsh every spring since before you were born, and before that I helped my father burn it off—I ought to know what I'm doing," said Harmon. "Hand me more rags and stand back." He unscrewed the top of his gas can, doused a tee shirt Jude handed him, and knelt just outside the willow copse. "You might wonder why we need rags and gasoline when it's so dry—I'm surprised you haven't opened your big mouth about that. Well, it's because grass burns funny if you try lighting it just by itself. It's sort of like a stick of dynamite—it takes a wick to set it off right." He struck a wooden match against the side of his shoe. The rag lit with a whoosh. Harmon leaped back and then lunged forward to feed bundles of grass into the flame. This hardly proved necessary.

Smoke from the burning tee shirt was gray. When the grass ignited, it turned brown and white, and as the heat and flames intensified, it took on a steamy yellow tinge near the ground. The fire manufactured a wind of its own, soon a hot wind howling out toward the river, just as Harmon predicted. It crackled around his knees, licked at both their feet, then exploded out into the grassy mat that lay before them like a carpet from a hundred-acre roll.

"Whew!" said Harmon, brushing his knees, "I've never seen a fire take off like this one."

They moved quickly away a hundred feet or so where Harmon asked for another rag. Jude handed him a pair of wrestler's trunks with the seat torn out.

"You should have seen what a mess I made of the bastard who did this," chortled Harmon, recalling a match twenty years ago.

At the moment, Jude couldn't think of anything but this fire. A hundred feet further along the edge of the willow copse, he handed him more underwear, and then yesterday's tee shirt, mostly fern green. *Whoosh! Whoosh!* continued the tiny explosions of gasoline and rag with Harmon dancing out of reach, no longer bothering to hand-feed grass into it. Fifteen minutes passed, and Jude's rag sack was nearly empty, having in it no more underwear than Harmon could have been wearing as he lunged clear of his latest explosion. As soon as the flames settled back and the smoke turned from gray to brown and white, he grabbed the sack from Jude and tossed it in along with the last of his underwear.

"That ought to do it," he said. "I told you I knew all about this job."

Jude couldn't deny it. Though an awesome holocaust was developing out into the widest part of Harmon's marsh, all of it had stayed safely to the willow side of the tree farm, and all of it was spreading out toward the river. He couldn't see a red-winged blackbird anywhere now, nor could he really see much of the flame. Brown and white smoke billowing toward the river filled the blue sky and obscured nearly everything beneath, and even as he stood upwind from it, amazed at the colossal proportions of this thing he helped create, a bit of the smoke cloud made him cough, for a back draft of some sort had just eddied their way.

Nothing burns like dry grass, the substance of which when it curls into a mat under the weight of winter snow is still mostly air, so much air and so little fuel that the fire must race to keep itself burning. Sometimes even its flames seem unable to keep up. The obvious flames of a grass fire lie mostly in its wake where the worst of the burning isn't any longer. Its steadiest fire is the tedious consumption of rotting logs, old fence posts, and green willow wood in its aftermath. But where grass alone burns there is an almost instantaneous conversion of fuel into smoke, a flame erupting and then vanishing as fast as it erupted before erupting further on. It's like a tongue flicking from a mouth opening and closing and opening again. Only the smoke persists, this day to cast its hulking shadow like a dark afterthought over the river and the extensive network of wild grasslands that lay out of reach beyond it. The sun had by this time sunk into treetops on Miss Thorpe's hill, darkening the smoke's underside and lightening it like a fleecy summer cloud on top.

"Let's go," said Harmon, pulling Jude out of what seemed like a trance with a tug on his shirtsleeve.

They walked back along the willow copse as far as the ravine entrance. When they reached the river bed, Harmon turned a last time to admire the blackened corridor through which his fire had sped out into the main part of his marsh. In the pride of his accomplishment, he couldn't help lecturing Jude a bit more. "See," he said, "even if the wind shifted back this way, the fire would only burn itself out. It wouldn't have anywhere to go, my boy, because everything back this way is already burnt. That's the way they fight fires, you know, by starting another fire in its path. Fight fire with fire—ever hear of that?"

Jude nodded.

"Those willows"—he gestured toward those nearest the tree farm ridge—"will never even get warm."

They followed the river back into the ravine, circling out of sight of the marsh, and climbed up from nearly night down there into twilight in the park above. In Harmon's van with its headlights flashing across tree trunks as they swerved one way and another, they navigated through the park aiming for an open space between the Bass and the Rabbit and out to the sandy road on the Rabbit's driveway. Harmon hummed a self-satisfied hum. Out on the sandy road he turned toward the far end of the park and soon they were bounding up Miss Thorpe's old driveway.

"I want to take one last look," said Harmon. "You can see nearly everything from up here, which you might have known already if you'd done what I told you last fall." He figured his fire would be burning itself out along the river by this time, and he felt another lecture coming on before he let go of Jude this day.

Even before they lurched over the last ruts and dodged the last tree roots and boulders to the crest of the hill, they could see an orange, aurora-like ring spanning the sky over the lands below. Harmon braked abruptly alongside the Woodcock, snapped off his headlights to have a better look, and opened his mouth to say something extremely self-satisfied. Instead he gasped in unison with Jude, about the only time they ever agreed.

"My God!" he said, horror-struck. "It's burning in the tree farm!"

To Jude it looked like the whole world was on fire.

23

Game Over

Had they walked along the entire length of the willow margin setting off gasoline explosions the whole way, what came to be called *The Great Hawkers Marsh Fire* might never have happened. But Harmon used up most of his underwear and all of his enthusiasm for the job before he got quite that far, and as the fire raced toward the river, it had angled slightly away from the willows, leaving itself a narrow bridge of grass to burn back upon when the wind shifted—as it had. Far down on the other end, the blaze had circled back from the river, exploded through the willow copse, and jumped the ridge. The Christmas trees of Johnson and Faber were igniting like Roman candles. Jude must have seen a hundred flare up in the five seconds they watched in dumbfounded silence from the hilltop.

They were too far away to see that the fire had already spread out of the tree farm on one side, into an adjacent section of marsh not belonging to Harmon, and even as they sat there, was jumping the pitifully narrow river upstream from the ravine and from there booming out into grasslands beyond it in three directions, a matted carpet of old slough hay and brush extending all the way to Twin Rivers in the freshening wind's new course.

Grinding his teeth as much as his gears, Harmon backed his van around and careened down Miss Thorpe's driveway with Jude's head twice thumping against the roof. Since Harmon's phone wasn't yet connected for the summer season, they raced up the sandy road to Twisters to call for help. Jude noticed Phyllis' school bus parked alongside the Perch.

"I should tell my mother where I am," he said. "I'm late for supper."

"No time to stop now," muttered Harmon. "If you want to jump out, go ahead for all I care."

Jude didn't think much of jumping out at the seventy miles an hour they were doing just then. It seemed like a better idea, though not a very good one, to go with Harmon to Twisters where the skinny man, the state fire warden, stood behind the lunch counter lighting a cigar as they charged in. Across from him sat Carl Connors puffing a half-smoked cigar. Behind them playing *Wild Card* and also puffing a cigar was a Twin Rivers High senior who sometimes worked at the gas station next door.

The skinny man sucked on his cigar, pulled it out, and fondly examined the lit end of it. "Carl's wife just had twin girls," he said.

"And all hell has broke loose," said Harmon.

"Sometimes it seems that way to me too," said Carl dreamily, "but we'll get along if my mother-in-law will help out. Here, have a cigar, Harmon." He pulled one from his shirt pocket. Another came with it and rolled down the counter toward Jude. "You have one too," he said to Jude.

Harmon pushed away his cigar. "We've got to call for help," he shouted at them all. "A fire burnt out of my marsh, and now it's in the tree farm. We've got to stop it before it gets out of control."

The senior quit playing *Wild Card* with two pinballs left in his game. Carl swung around on his stool. His lips formed a tight circle around his cigar butt, a stubby black butt from which a gray ash drooped. He needed a few seconds to clear his brain of problems like who was going to change all those diapers and how he was going to squeeze twins into his pickup.

"If the tree farm is burning, it's already out of control," he said slowly as if each word was a number in a column he was attempting to add.

"And you're a damn fool for starting it, Harmon," whined the skinny man.

"And you're a damn fool for issuing me the permit," Harmon struck back.

"I'll call the State Forestry people on my CB radio," Carl said. "Radio is great for emergencies like this." He jumped from his stool excited as a watchdog now.

The skinny man hurried into a backroom to call the Twin Rivers Fire Department. Harmon laid a limp hand on Jude's shoulder, a hand that felt like a gasoline-soaked rag and nothing at all like Harmon's hand as Jude recalled it from the night he came to supper. Carl Connors and the Twin Rivers High senior raced out the door.

"You run down to my place on the double," Harmon said to Jude in a low voice. He took out a large key ring and from that the key to his cabin. "I'm going to need my burning permit for sure. It's on top of the refrigerator, under the clock. Get it, and come back here fast, because in a few minutes lots of people will want to see it." He handed Jude the key. "It was all legal." He seemed to chew on *legal*. "I haven't done anything wrong." He chewed on *wrong*. "On top of my refrigerator," he said again as Jude turned to leave.

Had Jude any chance to think about it, he might have found it strange to be racing down the sandy road on a rescue mission for Harmon Grove. He might have found it equally strange to be groping in the dark for the Pike's light switch, just as he'd done for Miss Thorpe's in a time suddenly far away. He found Harmon's burning permit under the clock, a white slip folded in two with the skinny man's signature scrawled across the back of it. As it happened, the clock's hands at the half hour seemed to be pointing to more than the time, for immediately in front of it on top Harmon's refrigerator in several loose swirls shimmered Miss Thorpe's silver cross and chain.

On his way outside, Jude came face-to-face with *Alarmin Harmon*, not the wrestler himself, but an old poster on the inside of Harmon's door, curling from one corner where it had torn loose from its tack, advertising an event *Coming Soon!* more than twenty years ago now. Harmon glistened all over, as if he had worked up a dreadful sweat or just stepped out of the shower into bright sunshine. He wore wrestling trunks only, perhaps the same ones Jude had fished from the paper sack less than an hour ago. His black boots might have been bolted in place. He had three times as much hair, most of it hanging in his face, and seemed twice the size he was these days, much larger than the Harmon he had left behind at Twisters ten minutes ago, a man now shrinking rapidly. Under each bulging bicep he held the head of a hapless opponent whose arms dangled limp as the untied laces of their wrestling boots from which Harmon seemed about to yank them.

Displaying a monstrous grimace, at any moment he would bang their heads together. Beneath the picture, large letters proclaimed: *SHOWS NO MERCY, ASKS FOR NONE!*

Jude turned out the light and ran next door to the Perch. Phyllis Cobb, who was just leaving, stood outside on the stoop talking to his mother through the screen door.

"You're late for supper," Kate said. "Where have you been?"

"Debby Connors had twins this morning," Phyllis interrupted. "So your mom has a job if she wants it."

Both of them stared at the cigar sticking out from Jude's shirt pocket.

"The tree farm is on fire," he said pointing to an orange glow in the sky above the ravine. Faintly in the air around them was the smell of smoke.

Seconds later they were all riding up to Twisters in the school bus. Both Harmon's van and Carl Connors' pickup were gone from the parking lot. Two deep wheel marks scarred the gravel where Carl's truck had been. The café was open, but even the skinny man, locking the cash register, was on his way out. "They've probably all gone to either Johnson's or Faber's," he shouted over his shoulder to Phyllis and Jude while Kate waited in the bus.

"A logging trail leads into the tree farm from both their yards. Maybe we'll catch up with them there," said Phyllis as she climbed back into the bus, closing the door before she remembered Jude was still inside the café.

Carl Connors' other cigar lay on the lunch counter where Harmon had left it, and sputtering on *Wild Card*, which Jude shoved in walking out, was the senior's unfinished game. It tilted. *Game Over* flashed out sequentially one letter at a time.

What followed was a fire that no one in the North Crow River Country would ever forget, least of all Harmon who started it by burning his old underwear and would have wanted to forget, and Jude who helped him and had every reason to remember it. Before sunrise of the first day it had entirely blackened the five hundred acre Christmas tree farm. By sunset on its third and final day it had run through the river marshes and neighboring woods and brushlands two-thirds of the way from Hawkers Park to Twin Rivers. Along its path, a hundred secondary fires had burnt, heading off in directions of their own. Its smoke and ash fell upon Twin Rivers and choked its schools and most of its businesses into closing for the day.

It choked Mr. Desmond Willoughby, or at least he thought it did as he cocked an eye toward the grimy heavens outside his principal's office window. Smoke would sicken his vitals, he fretted, and then—checking himself— he tried thinking low blood pressure types of thoughts. He raised and lowered his eyelids by fractions. He sat down at his desk, pushed his chair back, and crossed his legs. Closing the high school today created confusion, so he and the superintendent had delayed the decision as long as possible. Now activities had to be re-scheduled, meetings re-arranged, the school calendar revised, announcements made over the intercom. Mr. Willoughby hated announcements. He hated excitement and smoke. He swallowed a shot of stomach antacid.

In an otherwise empty faculty lounge, Mr. Evanson moped with no one to share his dismay over a geometry test he'd pointlessly spent last evening preparing and now had to postpone. He hadn't heard the school closing announcement on his car radio driving in that morning. He hadn't even bothered to turn it on. The air, it seemed to him, had cleared a bit overnight. Mr. Evanson was the sort who trusted the evidence of his senses. The day seemed brighter, albeit not very bright, and so he only discovered his mistake when he found himself alone in the staff parking lot, save for Mr. Willoughby's car in the principal's space.

Having stayed up later than usual and then gotten up at his usual time, having skipped a breakfast he usually skipped, having come this far already, Mr. Evanson's unexpected day off was already ruined as far as he was concerned. He wasn't interested in fighting fires. Fighting indifference in the classroom was his role. There was always enough of that every year when April rolled around, and now with his classes cancelled, there would be more indifference than ever to contend with. He suppressed a yawn, looked around for a newspaper, and wondered if it would be worth it to make a pot of coffee.

The fire brought to its thirty-mile perimeter such distant people from Jude's world as Mr. Port, the school librarian, and George Cobb, captain of two dozen pea-green earth loaders. Here was Clarence, hired man of Cobb Construction, with tobacco bulging in his cheek. Miss Greshmer wore tennis shoes, hardhat, and gray smudges on her acne as she stood along the Twin Rivers highway behind two coffee jugs on a folding table. Kate and Phyllis and hundreds of others dug trenches with garden spades. Carl Connors fanned the flames—in his heart at least he fanned them and regretted their ever dying. He wagged his CB antennae tails over roads where he never stopped moving long enough to extinguish a spark. He loved excitement. His dust, in clouds behind his pickup, was indistinguishable from smoke.

Helicopters circled the skies towing enormous buckets of water dipped from lakes. Airplanes spewed blue-green clouds of flame retardant. Carl tried to radio the helicopters. With his lips to his crackling mike he shouted directions.

"Drop it here!" he screamed. "Drop it there!" Do you read me, old buddies?"

But the helicopters were as unconcerned as dragonflies, even if they *read* Carl, and even though he called them *old buddies* on every one of his forty channels. They buzzed away to drop their loads on other heads than his, excitement Carl would miss. He chased after them. He wanted to see water drop from three hundred feet. He wanted to see it splash.

Meanwhile, a hundred times Harmon pulled from his shirt pocket the burning permit signed by the skinny man, and at least that many times the skinny man said it was legal at the time he issued it, but he had cautioned Harmon about starting a fire.

The day Twin Rivers High School cancelled classes Jude worked on the fire line with Ronny Faber and Peter Johnson whose houses would have burnt but for some well-placed helicopter water buckets. At day's end, the three of them laid down their shovels, gulped Miss Greshmer's coffee in steamy swallows, ate salami sandwiches, and talked together like lifelong friends. And all that time, for three days, whether he was near the fire or far from it, whether wielding a shovel or trying to get some sleep, there burnt within Jude's pocket like an ember of the blaze the silver cross he'd taken from Harmon's cabin.

24

The Villain and the Hero

A week before the fire, Jude had seen the first sign of Miss Thorpe in the four months since she moved from the park, her name in the entertainment section of the Twin Rivers *Daily Dispatch* where an advertisement listed 'Jeannie T' as an attraction at Dwyer's Purple Palace.

"And this could be good news or bad, depending on how you look at it," said his mother. "She has a job, but it can't be much of one in a place like that, and when Harmon reads about it, he'll probably try getting a court judgment against her wages."

"We're not going to tell him, are we?" Jude asked later on when the cabin lights were out, and he had gone to bed on the sagging couch.

"It may come as a surprise to you, Jude, but the man can read," said his mother from her room where a lamp was still lit. She got up and stood in the doorway. A match flared as she lit a cigarette. "*We* won't have to tell him."

Even had Harmon read it the night Jude did, Miss Thorpe needn't have worried. During the three days of the fire, he was the most preoccupied man Jude had ever seen—the most fumbling, beset, and thoroughly fretted man. He alternately attacked the inferno and viewed it with an almost morbid detachment. Sometimes he would seem to be everywhere at once along the fire line, directing traffic, shouting encouragement, and with his face as black as a coal miner's driving a Cobb Construction bulldozer. At other times, he appeared to regard the spectacle as if he were merely an awed passerby. He quit being all apology, explanation, and effort. He would stand off by himself somewhere gaping. Once when Jude caught his eye at such a moment, Harmon seemed not to recognize him.

"Did they really close the schools today?" he asked, stupefied and incredulous, as if waking from a dream, and apparently not realizing that he spoke to Jude Henley from the next-door cabin in his park, Jude who had helped him lose his rent money and start the fire, a boy who needed a father to set him straight.

Already there was talk Harmon would be named in a hundred lawsuits; that court judgments and the like would be brought against *him*; that he ought to be arrested and thrown in jail. Jude first heard this when he was resting with Peter and Ronny near the P.T.A. volunteer refreshment stand where Miss Greshmer worked. Harmon doddered by with a Styrofoam cup of coffee in one hand, a shovel in the other, and for the moment a dazed expression on his face. He might have been sleepwalking through a nightmare.

"He'll be a long time hearing the last of this," said Peter, pointing venomously at his back. "Oh, baby, will he get what's coming to him! My dad says he'll have him in court as soon as this is over. We'll have the shirt off his back, maybe even wind up owning Hawkers Park, and you, Jude, will be our star witness. Oh, baby oh!"

Harmon's wasn't much of a shirt, and somehow Jude took little comfort from the thought of Peter taking Harmon's place in the park. Peter becoming his landlord hardly seemed an improvement.

Just then he laid his arm on Jude's shoulder. During the fire, they'd become friends—at least from Peter's viewpoint. Jude couldn't help being suspicious of any change as sudden as this. Though things had remarkably improved for him in school since that terrible day his name appeared alongside *The Joys of Motherhood,* though he now had the best grade in geometry class and might finish the year on the school honor roll, between Peter and him especially there persisted a feeling they were on the verge of another fight. Sometimes as Jude fell asleep on the sagging couch, he would entertain himself with thoughts of pulverizing Peter, something he was sure he could do if it came to that. While he had grown a half foot since last September, Peter seemed to have shrunk and now couldn't see over his shoulder, so it wasn't easy for him to keep his arm there for long. Jude saved him the trouble by taking a step toward Miss Greshmer's refreshment stand.

Only yesterday Peter held a seat for him on the back of the school bus, shouting for him as he climbed aboard, "Hey, Jude, back here!" Peter had smuggled on the bus a can of orange soda, which he slipped from his shirt pocket as Jude sat down beside him. He invited Jude to have the first drink. Was this friendship or had Peter's father instructed him to take good care of the *star witness*?

Their bus had been sent home early yesterday because of heavy smoke near the Twin Rivers highway and reports that it might have to be barricaded. Over the school inter-com Principal Willoughby had announced with a shaky voice the possible cancellation of all Friday classes and ac-tivities. This brought a cheer in Jude's fourth hour study hall where simultaneously all eyes turned to him as if he were the one to thank for the prospect of a holiday. So on the bus ride home euphoria had mixed with a thrilling sense of emergency.

Soon other pop cans appeared, front and rear, and Phyl-lis, who must have noticed, for once didn't object when her rules were broken. Nobody seriously expected that the fire would spread into Twin Rivers and burn down the school, but still it might, it *just might*, thought the jubilant students on Phyllis' bus, and Jude was the one to thank.

"We'd sure get out early for summer vacation," chortled Ronny, beaming Jude's way. "Good old Jude!" He slapped him on the shoulder.

It seemed as if Harmon was blamed for everything bad resulting from the fire, and Jude credited with everything good for having helped him light it. Harmon had overnight become the neighborhood fool, Jude its hero as the only witness to his folly. Twice already the sheriff had ques-tioned him about it with a deputy standing by recording his answers. "Good work," the sheriff had said, also slapping him on the shoulder. He'd been slapped and patted, shoul-der and back, a hundred times since the blaze began, by people he knew and complete strangers. Instead of being in the middle of the pack where he always wanted to be, he had been hoisted up on the pack's shoulders and was being carried around in something resembling a parade.

A Twin Rivers *Daily Dispatch* photographer took his picture, which was printed on the front page alongside one of Harmon, the skinny man, and several others talking with the sheriff. A single caption under both pictures read in part, *Sheriff probes cause of the great Hawkers Marsh fire ... Cause* appeared directly beneath Harmon's feet. The accompanying article described Jude as a witness crucial to the investigation.

Settling back with his cup of coffee now, Mr. Evanson in the faculty lounge, newspaper spread out on the table in front of him, tapped his index finger precisely upon Jude's picture. Here was a boy who would amount to something someday, classroom clock rescuer and now his prize geometer. Certainly, as Jude's teacher, he had a hand in this somewhere. *Harmon Grove*? Where had he heard that name before?

Miss Thorpe, who had read the same story, had nothing to fear from Harmon for the time being and probably forever after, nor had Jude much to fear for retrieving her silver cross from his cabin. Two days had passed with Harmon near enough to strangle him a dozen times at least, and Jude prepared to be strangled—if it came to that—rather than hand it over. Instead he couldn't have said whether Harmon noticed or even cared to think about it if he happened to notice.

Equally unexpected was to find pity for Harmon nudging in even as fear of him drifted away. That burdensome inheritance from his father, his sense of justice, must have been the source of it. He might have enjoyed the sight of Harmon tortured a little, but it went much too far to have him hung and spinning from the end of a rope, which is where he seemed headed in most people's thoughts. Even if the more likely outcome were bankruptcy and a ruined reputation, that too seemed extreme.

Wasn't he almost as much an arsonist as Harmon? Aren't accomplices equally implicated in crimes? And was he not—by some standards at least—a liar and a thief? He didn't want blame and was happy that none came his way, but he didn't want credit either. He wished he wasn't on the front page—though he liked thinking Miss Thorpe might have seen him there.

He'd always been the kid out of sight in the middle somewhere. In the middle of the row, in the middle of the bus, in the middle of the alphabet—that's the way he wanted it. He hadn't wanted to be a witness against Miss Thorpe, so he lied. Now he didn't want to be a witness against Harmon.

"Just tell them what happened, just tell them the truth," his mother had said.

What happened? The truth? It all sounded so simple, yet it turned out to be so hard. Telling the truth was no simpler than lying. Nothing stayed where you left it. Once you let go, it was like a fire burning somewhere out of control. You never knew where it might go, what it would do, and where it might lead you.

25

Smoke Get in Your Eyes

Toward the end of the fire's last day, Jude slipped away from Peter and Ronny and strangers slapping him on the back. With the blaze burning itself out in river marshes far from the highway on both sides, he hitchhiked into Twin Rivers. The early evening sun was slipping behind a deep gray overcast everyone took for smoke and nobody dared think might be rain on the way.

His experience gave him new respect for Phyllis' theory about weird people picking up hitchhikers. It might not have applied to George, but it certainly fit the family of sightseers who offered him a ride this time. They had driven out from Twin Rivers in a three-seater station wagon to see the blackened countryside firsthand, the most impressive parts of which were not to be seen from the highway. They were all disappointed, especially a little girl Jude sat beside in the third seat, shared as well by an uncontrollable puppy and the little girl's grandmother who kept her head low and her face in a flowery pocket handkerchief the whole time.

"Where's the fire, anyway?' asked the driver, apparently the father of the family. "Gram so wanted to see the fire. Darn though!"

"Most of what's left of it is on the other side of those trees," Jude shouted up to him as they sped toward Twin Rivers, too fast to see anything very well regardless.

"Darn though!" the man shouted back to Jude. "Gram, do you hear? He says most of the fire's beyond those trees." The man gestured at trees streaming by in a blur. The car swerved.

Gram, with her head bent down below the window, kept her face in her handkerchief, didn't seem to care.

"Gram, do you hear?" The man had a whining way with his words, a nostrilly singsong sounding like baby talk.

Gram croaked something into her handkerchief, a few muffled syllables Jude couldn't interpret, though it seemed she was more concerned about inhaling smoke than seeing anything that might be seen. The uncontrollable puppy danced around his feet, its sharp teeth tearing at his socks, scratching his ankles.

"How many people were killed?" the little girl asked Jude. She had been picking her nose and studying the results on the tips of several fingers.

"Nobody was killed that I know of," Jude replied, but it was a mistake to say so, for at once she began to kick her feet and cry. Jude pushed the puppy from his ankles.

"Daddy promised me we would see dead bodies," the little girl sobbed. "I want to see some yucky dead bodies."

"Another time, dear," shouted Daddy from behind the wheel.

Gram laid a bony hand as white as limestone on the little girl's convulsing knee, and as she did so, the puppy leaped and ripped away the handkerchief dangling from her sleeve. The little girl slapped Gram's hand away, the puppy rolled on the floor with her handkerchief, and Jude was let out in front of an all but deserted Twin Rivers High, the first thing he could think of when he was asked where he was going and the farthest thing from his mind.

From there he walked downtown and then through the shabby section beyond it. A smoky haze hung over Twin Rivers streets, making no distinction between good neighborhoods and bad, mixing an aroma like that of a thousand burnt suppers with the strangely sweet smells of city filth and springtime. As is often the case when it comes to thought as opposed to action, the closer Jude got to his destination, the slower he walked. What had seemed so straight-forward and simple an hour ago when he stood on the shoulder of the Twin Rivers highway looking for a ride, began to require more thought than the great amount of thought he'd already devoted to it. The slower he walked, the more he found to think about. The more he thought about, the more he hesitated.

This went on for several Twin Rivers blocks until at last he stood under a purple canvas marquee while lightning flashed and rain pattered overhead giving him a convenient reason for standing there. A sign in a chrome frame one side of the Purple Palace entrance said, *Jeannie T Nightly at the Piano*. Since he hadn't known she played the piano in addition to her singing, this gave him yet another reason to pause. Perhaps his mother was right when she said he didn't really know Miss Thorpe. She was just someone in his mind and not at all like who she really was.

He bent to study her picture on the sign as if that might help. Looking up from a keyboard, she faced the camera. She appeared to be singing, but she might have been simply smiling. Jude thought of last autumn and everything that had happened to him since he first heard her name. People leaping from bridges are said to have their whole lives flash before their eyes. Jude's life of the past eight months seemed to flash before his. It was enough to make him change his mind and go home, which he might have done except for a man shoving him aside and turning to confront him at precisely that instant.

"So what are you up to?" Dusty Dwyer demanded.

Thunder rolled away over their heads. There was no going back.

"Miss Thorpe," Jude stammered before he could consider how dumb it sounded.

Dusty Dwyer pretended to be puzzled. His amusement was genuine. "Who ever heard of *Miss Thorpe* around here?" He nodded toward the sign. "If it's Jeannie T you're looking for, she better be playing now in the lounge. Your Miss Thorpe makes me think I hired a school teacher. Are you a friend of hers?"

Jude nodded. He was Miss Thorpe's friend.

"You're a little young for her, if you ask me. I didn't know she collected toy boys," Dusty said with a smirk. His straight black hair, streaked with gray, fell over the collar of the white turtleneck he wore inside a light blue shirt open three buttons down from his collar. He chewed gum in the same slow rhythm with which he jangled loose change in his pocket and tossed around ideas in his head. "Is it important?"

Jude nodded again.

"Real important!"

He swallowed hard and nodded again.

"You don't say much, do you?"

"I guess not," said Jude.

"Okay, come on in—I don't mind."

On other days Dusty might have minded, but today he was in his best mood. The fire had been good for business. Every night of it his nightclub had been packed with fire-fighting customers looking for entertainment between shifts on the fire line. Tonight, it would be packed again. You would have thought it was a party, not the disaster it was made out to be. The firefighters talked loud, drank fast, and threw their money around, much of it Buster's way. They brought smoke in with them, so much smoke that the Palace smelt like a barbecue, but Dusty didn't mind that either.

"But don't hang around," he said to Jude as he pushed him toward the door. "Get out before my girl starts her next dance act, do you hear? That should begin about eight, and it's half past seven now, so that's how much time I'm giving you. Thirty minutes you've got. That's all, and don't try buying any booze—I don't want trouble with the law for letting kids hang around my place. Do you know what I mean?"

He pointed to a decal on the door frame, the head of a policeman, half a head really, with his left ear and eye having peeled away, and with a detached hand from a missing arm raised alongside in a stopping gesture and the words below it: *Positively No Minors Allowed!*

Rain pattered more insistently on the purple marquee. Its loose edges flapped in a gusting wind. Thunder rolled across the sky as Dusty pushed him into a purple-carpeted foyer where three arched entrances led into areas of his nightclub. He then stepped in front to face him again where a coat check room was wedged like a pie slice between two of the arches.

"I said, *do you know what I mean*?"

Jude nodded. In a strange way, Dusty Dwyer reminded him of his geometry class and Mr. Evanson asking him to repeat a lesson. He might have been expected to say *the sum of the parts cannot be greater than the whole.*

"A half hour, no booze," he said instead. His fingers inside his pocket tangled themselves in the fine chain of the silver cross.

Rain lashing against windows in the foyer created brown rivulets running more sideways than down. Dusty stepped aside and gestured toward the coat check in a manner displaying more suspicion than courtesy. Dusty wanted the whole world in front of him where he could keep an eye on it; so did Mr. Evanson.

"She'll tell you where your *Miss Thorpe* is," he said. He pointed toward a bare-shouldered blonde girl slouching at a counter. Sagging away from her pink lips was the smile she'd just given Dusty Dwyer. Her cheeks bore spots of rouge, the one on the right so much higher that it gave her face a lopsided look.

"What do you want?" she asked Jude.

"He's looking for our piano player," shouted Dusty over his shoulder as he disappeared through one of the arches.

Jude didn't need directions since piano sounds plinked from the archway farthest to his left, and then—startling him, even though he might have expected it—he heard Miss Thorpe singing for the first time since last fall, not one of her old songs he practically knew by heart, but a song so new he'd heard it earlier in the week on Phyllis' school bus radio which she always played while they were boarding and turned off the minute they were underway.

"Normally I'm not supposed to let kids in there," said the coat check with a gesture toward the same archway.

"Dusty says it's okay."

"Dusty? I'll *bet* you call him Dusty, just like one of his best buddies. You look about seventeen to me, and you smell like smoke. Is the fire still burning?"

Jude felt precious time slipping away, but it was flattering to be thought seventeen when he would only be sixteen next summer. "It's almost out now," he said of the fire. "This rain will take care of it for sure." For good measure, he added that he'd been helping to fight it. He stepped toward the piano bar archway. Though he did his best to look confident, his heart thumped and his legs wobbled while his feet felt glued to the Palace's thick carpet.

"I'll just bet you put the fire out all by yourself," teased the coat check girl with a not unfriendly tone, and then noticing Jude's hesitation in the archway she added, "Jeannie's right in front of your nose. Go on in."

In front of Jude's nose stretched a long row of dark wood tables, all with red glass lanterns burning on them and mostly men sitting around them, grinning, gesturing, talking, and smoking, or otherwise silent men alone with heads bowed almost prayerfully staring into drinks cupped in their hands. Faces in the dancing candle flames were as orange as sunset. Alongside these tables ran a bar where practically nobody sat at the hour Jude came in, the hour of the evening's first show which could be seen from there in a mirror running its length. Later, during Buster's strip show, the bar stools were usually full, with men watching her with their backs to her, from the safe distance the mirror provided. It was a way of being there and not exactly being there, which worked out better for some men, George Cobb among them who always sat at the bar on the end nearest the archway where Jude now stood.

In the bar mirror, he caught his first glimpse of Miss Thorpe. For him too it was a way of being there and not being there. She sat before a white baby grand piano on a moon-shaped stage elevated into an alcove with a gold braided rope strung across the front of it. Two red glass lanterns burnt on her piano. She wasn't far from him but getting to her would have taken him past all the tables up to the stage in full view of everyone. So he hung back inside the archway looking at her in the mirror while she used a microphone to introduce her next song.

"As a thank you to all the firefighters," she said, "this oldie." And she began singing *Smoke Gets in your Eyes*, which of course Jude recognized from his vigils behind her cabin. Her voice amplified through speakers in corners of the room, had some of that reedy quality he'd found in it when it first traveled out to him on that copper tubing running through her cabin wall. He still knew it by heart: its words didn't have much to do with fighting fires:

They asked me how I knew,
My true love was true,
I of course replied, something deep inside,
Cannot be denied.

The coat check girl touched his shoulder. "Look, you can't just stand here in the doorway gawking. Even if this song's for you, they'll throw you out."

They appeared to be a burly bartender in a vest of red sequins who was leaning wearily on his elbows behind the bar and looking big enough to be spoken of in the plural.

"What do you want here anyway? I'll see if I can help you." She pushed against him, close enough that he noticed both her perfume and a small mole on her left shoulder.

He said he had something belonging to Jeannie T.

"Give it to me—I'll get it to her."

"It's personal."

The coat check girl arched an eyebrow. "Write it down then, if that's the way you feel about it." Her small, icy hand in his led him away from the piano bar archway to where she found him a notepad. "Write down your message," she said. "I'll take it to Herm—he's the bartender and bouncer. He runs things in there when Mr. Dwyer isn't around. Herm will pass your note to Jeannie as soon as she breaks for Buster's next show. I'll put you down in there out of the way where you can wait for her. Otherwise you're going to get bounced. Believe me, Herm doesn't monkey around. In this business, you can't."

A stubby pencil kept slipping from his sweaty fingers as he leaned over the counter writing this message, trembling too obviously:

Miss Thorpe, I have to see you—important. He signed his name and added after it, *the boy from Hawkers Park*, because he wasn't sure she would remember him otherwise.

All the while the coat check girl had been reading over his shoulder. "Miss Thorpe? I never heard her called that before. Everyone around here calls her Jeannie. Are you sure you have the right gal?" She giggled. "The *boy*? Don't be so modest. You already told me what a *man* you are."

She led him back into the bar, past all the tables, to a booth around the corner, out of sight of most everything, the stage included. "Just wait here," she said. "Jeannie is about finished."

Rain and hail pelted the Purple Palace's roof.

"Hey, it's raining!" said the coat check girl.

"This will be the end of it for sure," said Jude with the fire in mind, though it might have applied to other things.

"I just love rain, and I hate this dry weather." She squeezed his hand once more and left him there. On her way back through the bar, she gave Jude's note to Herm at the service end. Despite her warning that Herm might throw him out, he had taken but sleepy notice of Jude whose note he stuffed into his vest pocket and resumed his leaning on the bar.

When your heart's on fire, you must realize,
Smoke gets in your eyes.

Miss Thorpe finished her song to applause not as loud as the rain had become. Seconds later she slid into the booth across from Jude.

"Hi, Jude Henley!" she said. She held out his note and laughed. "What's all this Miss Thorpe silliness? Where'd all that come from? I haven't been called that since I was a kid in Sunday school."

Jude felt his face growing warm. *You don't even know her. She would probably laugh if you called her that*—his mother's words were coming true. He hoped he wasn't blushing, but how do you stop that from happening? The harder you try, the worse it gets. Miss Thorpe was turning into a stranger. She looked exactly like the woman he thought he'd been protecting all these months, but she wasn't that woman. His mother had been right: he could now see that he didn't know her at all. What he knew was something in his imagination, something in his heart, different in many remarkable ways from the woman sitting across from him. It was enough to make him wince.

"I guess I wasn't sure what to call you," he said of his note.

"Don't worry about it. Most people call me Jeannie, a few people call me other things, but nobody calls me *Miss Thorpe*, except for my Sunday school teacher and now you." She laughed again, showing her teeth. "Hey, I saw your picture in the paper—that's exciting. I could use some of your publicity."

Jude gave up trying not to blush, but before he had to say anything about his picture and the fire, a cocktail waitress slid a coke in front of him. "From Luanne," she said and drifted away.

"Who's Luanne?"

"The check room girl," said Miss Thorpe. "Our number-one flirt—watch out for her."

Jude didn't know how to begin. Naturally he had rehearsed something, but it was something of the sort people who know each other say to each other. He sipped his coke.

Loud music, banjoes and guitars, twanged from the bar's speakers.

"Buster will be starting her act pretty soon. You probably should be running along," said Miss Thorpe. "Did old what's-his-name send you looking for me?"

"Who?" he asked though he knew she meant Harmon.

"The fat guy who rents the cabins. I saw *his* picture in the paper too."

"No, he doesn't know I'm here."

Around the corner from them a high, sandy-throated voice began squealing from somewhere offstage:

If you go down in the woods today,
You'd better not go alone.
It's lovely down in the woods today,
But better to stay at home.

"That's Buster beginning her act. It's really different from mine. She doesn't sing very well, but I put 'em to sleep and she wakes 'em up. You shouldn't be here, really. Matter of fact, neither should I, but it pays well."

"I need a volunteer from the audience," Buster screamed as she pranced onto what had become a stage with Miss Thorpe's piano wheeled to one side. "I need an *able* man."

Catcalls and hoots greeted this news, followed by a general commotion as a man was shoved toward the stage by his friends. It might have been the scene in Jude's geometry class last Halloween, a thousand years ago.

"Come on, don't be shy," squealed Buster. "It's picnic time for teddy bears. Don't you want to have a picnic with me?"

More hoots and a whistle.

"What's on your mind? Hurry now," said Miss Thorpe.

Jude reached into his jacket pocket and pulled out the silver cross. None of this was the way he imagined it would be.

For every bear that ever there was
Is gathered here for certain,
Because this is the day
The teddy bears are having their picnic.

In all this uproar, the hoots, catcalls, and whistles, now feet stomping on the floor of the stage, and through it all rain and hail blasting away over their heads, Jude could barely hear her say, "What's this all about?" as she fingered the silver cross and chain.

"It was in the pocket of the jacket you left hanging in your closet. Harmon Grove found it and was going to keep it till you paid him." Jude finished his coke and stared at her over the brim of his glass searching her face for recognition of a silver cross with turquoise insets, searching for recognition of his loyalty to her through all these months, searching for anything at all.

I'm your friend, he thought of saying to her. *I'm not the spy you thought I was.* But why do things like that sound so right when you're only thinking about them? Why are they so easy to say in your mind, and why do they sound so foolish when the moment comes to actually say them? Why had it become so hard to talk when months ago up on the hillside below her cabin, sitting there by her, he had thought he could say anything?

Picnic time for teddy bears.
The little teddy bears
Are having a lovely time today.
Watch them. See them.

General pandemonium exploded around the corner where the bar was filling with drenched firefighters while Buster sang on, dropping her clothes as she circled a man seated on the stage. The man on stage with her tried his best to look pleased, but missionaries being boiled in large pots might have looked happier. Banjoes twanged, feet stomped, and hands clapped in a rising tide. The whole place shook.

"This isn't mine," Miss Thorpe was saying. "I suppose that jacket belonged to somebody who rented the cabin before I moved in. I just left it behind the door in case they came back looking for it, never checked its pockets." She slid the cross and chain back across the table to Jude. She looked at him earnestly, sympathetically he might have thought. "I'm sorry," she said laying her hand over the top of his. "I hope you didn't go to any trouble on my account."

Any trouble on her account. He looked at her and managed a faint smile with no less effort than it had taken earlier to suppress a blush.

"Not yours?"

She shook her head, sadly it seemed.

Beneath the warmth of her hand, his fingers tangling in the silver chain rested there at what had become a journey's end unforeseen. He gazed at her hand, and below his, a swirl of the chain curling out from beneath glinting in candlelight on the tabletop. The sounds all around him, a din seconds before, had become for him a vast silence in which he and Miss Thorpe sat silently alone. He knew this was the end of it. This was what he would have left to remember. There wouldn't be more. No matter how much he had rehearsed what he might say to her, he couldn't say more. This he knew even before Dusty Dwyer's hand smacked down alongside theirs with its ruby pinky ring winking at him as if to mock the warmth he felt.

"What are you doing here during the show?" shouted Dusty over the banjo, the hoots, the rain and hail, over everything. "I told you to get to hell out of here before the show started. —That glass ..." He grabbed Jude's empty coke glass. "Was there booze in that glass?"

"It was only a coke, Dusty," said Miss Thorpe. "He came here to see me, and I kept him here too long talking. He's just leaving—we're done now."

"You bet he's leaving, and I don't care who he came to see." He pulled Jude from the booth. "—Not that way for Christ's sake!"

Jude had spun around the corner and seen much more of Buster than he'd ever heard about from George Cobb. Every stool along the bar was filled by men looking in the mirror. Dusty pulled him back by his jacket collar.

"I can't have you walking through there in front of everyone when Buster is hopping around in her birthday suit."

He dragged Jude back into a gloomy hallway, past some restrooms, to a fire exit with a ventilating fan clanking above it, chewing through air seasoned with kitchen grease and lavatory soap.

So don't go out in the woods alone, sang Buster from the moon-shaped stage. Her words, more shouted than sung, echoed shrilly in the hallway from a speaker dangling there.

"I hope you didn't go to any trouble on my account, and thanks again," Miss Thorpe sang out from somewhere in the smoky gloom behind him. Did he imagine her for an instant stepping into the hallway at the far end with her hand at her forehead as if shielding her eyes from a light that wasn't there?

None of this was the way he thought it would be. A door opened, and he was pushed into an alley.

"Come back when you're a little older, toy boy," said Dusty breathing heavily. "I won't mind at all then." He slammed the door.

Water cascaded from the Purple Palace downspouts, flooding the alley, swirling around Jude's shoes. Rain pounded on a dozen garbage can lids. A rat scurried behind them. Jude, instantly drenched, circled out of the alley into a parking lot alongside. Two men came running from there, angling across his path toward the Palace entrance. Since they had light at their backs and shadows across their faces, and since he wasn't noticing much anyway, he didn't recognize them until they were close by and the taller of them spoke.

"Damn me!" said George Cobb, grinning and rubbing his nose with water dripping down his face. "I told you that you'd come back here someday to see for yourself, but I didn't think it would be this soon."

"He's a regular little sinner," said Clarence, the hired man.

They all stood together now in the shelter of the marquee.

"What did you see in there, Jude, old boy? Did you see Buster?" George poked Clarence in the ribs. "I told him about Buster," he said, "told him so much that he couldn't wait to see her, I guess."

They both laughed, slapping their wet sides with water splashing in all directions.

Jude headed out toward the street. "I didn't see much, George," he said.

"Hey, Jude, where are you going?" said George. "Do you have a ride home?"

Jude shook his head. Rainwater trickled down into his eyes. It felt like tears as he rubbed it away. *The cross wasn't hers after all—was that what she told him?*

"Wait in my car," said George. "It ain't locked. Clarence and I are going to have a couple of drinks to celebrate the end of the fire. Just two drinks, Jude, about a half hour." He looked at his watch. "About nine o'clock we'll be heading out and I'll take you home. Damn me, Jude, if I'm not glad to see you though." He pointed toward the parking lot, toward his car on the far side of it.

Jude walked that way.

26

A Better Way to End

The rain, a torrent moments before when he stood with George and Clarence under the Purple Palace marquee, had become a light drizzle by the time Jude crossed the parking lot to George's car. He sat inside for about five minutes staring at a dashboard where flashing reflections chased each other along chrome trim. Some of these were lightning, some a neon sign, and some were cars passing in the street. Then he got out and stood beside the car in what had now become a mist. He didn't feel like sitting down anywhere. He couldn't get any wetter than he already was. He decided to go for a walk instead of waiting there with his clothes sticking to his skin. Behind him the Purple Palace's neon fountain spewed its fake water into a sodden night.

Here for Jude was one of those moments when the desire to start over and do it some other way runs headlong into the impossibility of ever doing it again. What follows is a mixture of despair and relief not unlike a mixture of smoke and springtime. Behind him the fountain flickered. Behind the fountain more lightning flickered.

Puddles wore reflections and pavement glistened. Water gushed into gutters at every intersection. The fire was over. The drought was over. Something within Jude seemed over as well, not a bad thing like fire or drought, but good to be putting behind him all the same if he could hang on to it long enough to keep it that way. It was slippery though, and no grip of his was yet strong enough. It twisted and turned as he struggled to get his thoughts around it, and with each twist and turn it became something else. Rain may have cleared the air of smoke but seeing Miss Thorpe hadn't yet achieved the same for Jude.

He wondered what she would mean to him after this. He knew for certain she wouldn't be a sad memory nor even a bitter memory. The mistakes were his, not Miss Thorpe's. She had never asked for this kind of help, only help when her car was stuck—that was all, and the end of it for her as it should have been for him. This was his mistake. Urged on by his dislike of Harmon and what his mother called a *sense of justice*, he had made himself her protector. Among other fantasies and daydreams during his lonely vigils on the far end of the park, this was probably the most unlikely: that she actually needed him and would one day acknowledge what he'd done for her. When people didn't expect your loyalty or even need it, you might not be wrong in giving it regardless, but you were wrong in expecting very much from them in return. He wished the cross had been hers though—it seemed like a better way for this to end.

Still, she must have noticed some of the trouble he'd gone through for her. Her hand on his and the look in her eyes said so. Hers had been a warm hand, and her look more puzzled than grateful, as if to ask why he had done it. Had she actually asked, he wouldn't have known what to say, so how could he expect her to understand when even he didn't? Already the past few months seemed like something happening in a dream, as if he had fallen asleep one afternoon on the hilltop last autumn, and only now awakened with supper waiting back home in the Perch. Or as if he'd fallen in love and then out again and was wondering how he could have been so foolish.

He had been warned that he didn't really know Miss Thorpe. Even George had warned him simply by being George, a guy you could look at it in different ways and in different lights, and depending on which way and how much light, either like him or think he was a jerk and maybe still like him regardless. George had told him *sooner or later he would have to see all sides.* When you got that far, what then? There might be lots of ways of looking at things, but eventually one would have to count for more than the others. Here too was a multiple-choice question. If it demanded an answer, if he didn't know what to do but had to do something, what could he do but guess?

A few blocks away and a few minutes later, he wandered into the neighborhood where his grandmother had lived. Trailing his feet by a few steps, his thoughts wandered much farther, into a time long ago when his father seemed almost to speak to him from pictures on her shelves and tabletops. Once more he heard his grandmother's rocking chair creaking and her soft humming. It was all there yet, somewhere behind him in what seemed a long journey to where he was now.

A child's red wagon full of rainwater had been left in his grandmother's front yard, a dog barked from its darkened porch, and a television flashed pictures from behind drawn drapes. People lived where he once lived. They would live in the park long after his time there. His grandmother never owned a television or a dog. Her privet hedge was gone. It all flashed by him, a jumble of memories and things he had hardly time to notice.

He ran five blocks to the public library.

"Psst, we're about to close," whispered an elderly librarian at the main desk as he swept by her.

"*Robinson Crusoe*," he said, out of breath, "Where would *Robinson Crusoe* be?"

She led him past rows of filing cabinets, past enormous old atlases laid out flat on tables, maps of the world, a globe which he left untwirled in passing, to rows of shelves at the rear of the building.

"We're really about to close for the evening," she said. "It's almost nine. You'll have to hurry. We seem to have three copies of *Robinson Crusoe*. It used to be a popular book, but people aren't the readers they once were. They miss a lot of the best things." She pulled all three copies from the shelf and handed them to Jude.

Through an open window nearby came the sound of water trickling from a downspout.

"If you want to check one out, make up your mind soon." She stepped away and closed the window, pulling a shade down over it. She went back to her desk in the front, pausing on her way to adjust an atlas on a table. Save for Jude, she had the library to herself at closing time.

Jude found the copy he wanted, the very book. He couldn't believe it as he walked away, having kept the library open ten minutes past closing while the librarian registered him as a new patron. On its borrower's card, he had discovered his father's signature in broad, black pencil strokes. Sixteen years later, only five names later on the card, he had been about to sign his own name beneath it, when the librarian fidgeting behind her desk interrupted him.

"No need to do that," she said. "These days it's all on the computer."

"That's my father," he said, pointing with his pen to the name higher up and signing his own below it anyway—with strokes broader and darker than he usually used.

"That's nice," said the librarian, as she scanned a bar-code and stamped a return date in his book. "Like father, like son, but next time try to get in here a little earlier, please."

It *was* nice, the nicest thing he could think of, for also in this book were short passages bracketed with those same pencil strokes, perhaps the very things his father read to his mother as he walked her home and almost ran into a lamp-post that afternoon many years ago. He would give *Robinson Crusoe* another try, this time with his father to guide him through it. He carefully slid the borrower's card back into its pocket.

"You can keep it if you want," said the librarian. "We just throw them away as we come across them now that we have computers. Your dad might get a kick out of it."

Jude didn't bother to say otherwise because in a way for him his father was more alive than he had ever been. Yes, his father would have gotten a kick out of it, and—who knows? —he might have imagined it this way. Dreamer that Jude was, he liked to think so.

He was fifteen blocks from the Purple Palace, twenty minutes late for George and Clarence, who shouted for him, waited around, and finally left without him. He hitchhiked home through the night, the rain, and a filmy haze which was all that was left of Harmon's fire. Under his jacket, held from the weather by an arm pressed against his chest (for the rain had begun in earnest again), was his father's *Robinson Crusoe* with bracketed passages, each one a message of some kind from the man he couldn't remember.

As he was walking drenched past Harmon's mailbox on the sandy road, he thought of the silver cross lying in the Purple Palace booth. He guessed it would make little difference to Harmon or anyone else. This time he guessed right at least where Harmon was concerned, but while Buster was finishing her act, Miss Thorpe had picked it up, tucked it carefully into folds of a handkerchief, and placed it in her purse.

A light glowed over the Perch's squeaky screen door. Rain dripping from its eaves formed glimmering blue rivulets either side. More rivulets ran up the driveway before vanishing in darkness where he stood. As if saying goodbye to something or someone, as if leaving rather than arriving, Jude glanced over his shoulder up the sandy road toward Twisters and the highway.

It had all begun with an orange bus and a yellow ball, and somehow the year had passed, and another summer spread out before him. Soon they would be moving from the park. He felt the book pressed against his chest. When he found what lay closest to his heart, he wouldn't have to guess any longer. He would know. Finally, he would know.

Acknowledgments

I wish to thank my wife Kate whose labors with this book in its most recent versions have been nothing less that an act of love. Her enthusiasm for the story with its array of characters and situations kept me going long after I might have set the work aside. My son David created the original Farhaven Press logo and provided invaluable assistance with a cover design incorporating my painting of a woodland scene reminiscent of Jude's world at Hawkers Park.

About the Author

James Casper was born and grew up in southern Minnesota. Apart from living in various Minnesota locales, he has resided in Boston, St. Louis, eastern Tennessee, and London, England where he is happiest walking from lock to lock along the Thames. He and his wife of twenty-four years have traveled extensively. Rome is one of their favorite places.

Website: http://farhavenpress.com/

More by James Casper

Everywhere in Chains is a moving story about a young girl whose real father's whereabouts is kept a secret to "protect her" from the truth. Ultimately, she is reunited with him, along the way proving that the path to healing takes a lot of courage and strength. The story provides a way forward for families who are victims of priest sexual abuse and for those who have a loved-one in prison. It has also been published in Poland as *Listy do Penelopy*.

An Accidental Pope takes you on a rollicking ride that ends with an accident filling the chair of St. Peter in Rome. There's never been an American pope. How might that change the world? Only one man will be chosen. But two murders in a row make the future unclear. Follow Harriet, an amateur sleuth, Porky White, a cop who uses juggling to help him think, a strip club owner who is rescuing women from the sex trade, and an unlikely pair of priests as mysteries unfold and justice is finally meted out.

And finally, if you like this book, please leave a short review online at Amazon or elsewhere. Your reviews really do help others decide if the story behind the cover might delight them, so it means the world to authors if you have something good to say. Thank you, from the team at Farhaven Press, Kate, James, and Henry the bulldog.

Compendium of the Catholic Catechism on Freemasonry

A Compendium on Theological and Historical Treatment on the Catholic Church's Prohibition Against Freemasonry and its Appendant Masonic Bodies

David L. Gray